JUST ONE KISS

Carole Dean

A KISMET™ Romance

METEOR PUBLISHING CORPORATION
Bensalem, Pennsylvania

Always Tim.
And Christine Hazenboom, my first reader.

CAROLE DEAN

Carole lives in British Columbia. Recently she became an island dweller and loves it. Every morning she wakes to the ever changing sound and colors of the ocean outside her window. Whatever its mood, summer calm or winter storm, she finds it the perfect background for writing romance. She lives with her husband of many years and a Rhodesian Ridgeback who has convinced them both he is a person in dog's clothing.

ONE

Nikki buzzed with energy. She had to go again. The snow was perfect. The runs were perfect. It just didn't get any better than this, and it would be weeks before she could come back. One more run. What could it hurt? She glanced toward the ski lifts—no line up. She would be at the peak in minutes.

"Nicole Johnson, don't even think about it. Come back to the chalet with us. You've been skiing like a madwoman all day. Besides, it's going to snow." Amy looked warily at the deepening gray of the sky, then back to her friend. "Not to mention there's probably not enough good light for another run."

"There's enough light. If there weren't, they wouldn't be operating the lifts. And it's for sure a little snow won't hurt. You cream puffs go to the chalet. I'm going back up. Without you to hold me up, I'll be down in no time," Nikki teased. "Unless some hardy soul wants to join me." She tossed one last dare at her three friends and coworkers.

"I may be a cream puff, but you, Niks, are crazy." Christy Coburn eyed the small group. "I'm for a hot drink. What about the rest of you?"

"Sounds good to me. I'm beat." John Zinnser pulled off his toque and shook it against his leg. As he stuffed it in his pocket, he glanced at Nikki. "Amy's right, you know. You should call it a day. You didn't even stop for lunch."

"You guys are worse than cream puffs. You're wimps." Nikki laughed. "We'll be locked in meetings for the rest of the weekend. This is the only chance we'll have to ski."

Amy pushed back her hat and loosened the zipper on her jacket. "If you must go, for heaven's sake, take it easy—and *don't* go all the way to the top. You're hungry and overtired, Nikki. Don't push yourself."

"Yes, Mother. Put the cocoa on. I won't be long." Nikki grinned and hurried to the lift.

Once on the chair, she turned to wave, but John and Christy were on their way to the lodge with its welcoming fireplace and warm drinks, and Amy's interest was elsewhere. She was talking to a tall, dark-haired man near the lift entrance.

When Nikki saw him bend to kiss her friend, her curiosity was piqued. Maybe Amy was holding out on her, she thought with a smile, craning for a better look. Try as she might, she couldn't make out his features. Blackcomb's high-speed lift, aptly named the Wizard, had already taken her too far out of range. Just as she turned back to look up the mountain, she noticed the man run to catch a chair. Another ski nut who can't resist the mountain, she thought. Confident Amy would fill her in on the stranger during après ski, Nikki settled in for the ride and let her thoughts turn elsewhere.

Tomorrow she was slated to make a presentation on behalf of her employer, Kingway Skin Care, to the company's new owner, Prisma International—plus a hundred or so distributors.

The takeover by Prisma last month was a complete

surprise. Even though Nikki agreed that the merger made good business sense—Prisma's cosmetics were, after all, the perfect complement to Kingway skin care products—there would be changes, and that made her edgy. Just thinking about a new boss gave her cramps.

Since her experience with her last employer, she put a high value on an employer who judged her solely on *job* performance.

Nikki couldn't think of the VAD situation, as she called it, without seething. She felt shame, too. Shame at being fired and raging anger at the injustice of it.

Ancient history, she told herself firmly and let the bad memory fade. But she would always be grateful to Amy Thurston for introducing her to Jayne Kingway. They hit it off instantly.

Working for Jayne was a treat. She was a true mentor, teaching, guiding, giving Nikki increasing responsibilities, and finally, just a year ago, promoting her to sales manager. Damn, she would miss her. Well, at least she'd be staying around for the next six months. That was some consolation.

When the invitation came for Kingway to make a presentation at Prisma's annual North American marketing meeting, Jayne chose Nicole as company spokesperson. "Impress the hell out of them," she'd said.

Tomorrow Nikki intended to do just that.

It helped that Whistler Village was the meeting site. Less than a two-hour drive from Vancouver, the resort was perfect for meetings intended to educate as well as reward office-bound executives. To a skier it was paradise, with a choice of two mountains boasting some of the best and longest runs in North America. To Nikki, it was also familiar. An avid skier who grew up near the mountains of Colorado, Nikki spent most free weekends at Whistler since moving to Vancouver.

Nikki was glad she didn't have to make this presentation in New York or Prisma's head office in Madrid. She shuddered a bit at the thought. Home turf was much more comfortable. Nikki usually had no trouble controlling her nerves, but every little bit helped.

A slight wobble in the smooth ride of the ski lift rocked her chair, distracting her from her thoughts. It righted itself and then, with a sudden abrupt lurch, stopped. Complete silence replaced the metallic purr of the lift as the chair swung aimlessly from the steel cable.

"Damn." Nikki spoke the word aloud, more in irritation than fear.

She'd spent enough time on lifts not to be afraid, but the sky was dark with clouds and she didn't relish freezing her bones on a teetering ski chair as the light faded further. In February, the winds were cold. She could only hope her blue jumpsuit would do its job. She was glad, too, that she was wearing the warm toque Amy had bought her as a joke in one of the local shops.

"Now this," Amy said when she discovered it, "makes a real fashion statement."

Nikki smiled. The hat was ridiculous. With three large pompoms dangling from its crown, each a different shade of screaming neon, its only statement was a giggle. Its base color was scarlet, a frightful match for her bright russet hair. When Amy dared her to wear it, she'd laughingly complied, knowing it was her friend's way of telling her to lighten up. *I guess I have been a bit of a Serious Sarah this last while,* Nikki admitted to herself. But there'd been so much to do.

"You okay?" A male voice came from behind her, faint but clear in the crisp mountain air.

"Fine. Thanks." She turned and yelled back. She couldn't see who asked the question. No matter. She didn't intend to get into a high decibel conversation three thousand feet up a mountain. Best to sit quietly and wait it out. She would use the time to review her presentation.

"Better get off at midstation. It looks like we're going to run out of light." The voice rose up to her again.

She acknowledged the advice with a wave of her hand but didn't answer back. She would make that decision for herself.

A gust of wind caught her chair from behind and pitched it roughly forward. It stabilized, but for a moment even Nikki's steely nerves weakened. This was no fun, no fun at all.

With a jolt, the ski lift started again.

Nikki sighed in relief as it began its rapid ascent to midstation. She wasn't wearing her watch, but she guessed about twenty minutes had passed. Most of the skiers ahead of her got off at the next station. Should she? She glanced up the mountain. Still enough light. She would go to the peak. Quickly, she transferred to the Solar Coaster, the chair that would take her to the T-bar lift and up toward the Blackcomb glacier.

Ignoring the lift attendant's look of disapproval, she switched chairs to carry on. He glanced at the sky and shrugged. Another cream puff, Nikki muttered to herself.

Alone at the top, she savored the solitude, the extravagant beauty and grandeur of the mountain. Blackcomb Mountain's vertical rise was 5,280 feet, one of the highest in North America. Magic Mountain, it was called. Up here, with her head touching the sky, Nikki felt that magic. The altitude gave a feeling of power, a psychological lift that said anything was possible. She wanted to save the feeling, hold it in reserve for those times when she needed it the most. Like tomorrow, she told herself.

She could have stayed at the peak forever, but she

was bold, not foolish, and neither the light nor the weather was in her favor. She pulled down her goggles, pushed a stray strand of hair haphazardly under the rim of the absurd hat, and tucked.

In seconds, she was flying down the mountain.

In minutes, she was piled up at the base of a tall hemlock.

TWO

The blackout couldn't have lasted more than a few seconds, but it was enough to disorient her. She struggled to respond to the deep male voice calling to her. But from where? She couldn't tell. The voice was closer now and it sounded angry. Why? Why was the voice angry? She stirred.

Michael Dorado couldn't figure out if he was concerned or annoyed. The foolish girl should have got off at midstation like he'd told her to. The damn lift was stalled over forty minutes, and it was getting colder and bleaker by the minute. Kids today, he thought in frustration, they never do what they're told! To top it off, she chose to go through Cougar Chute, an experts-only run and one of the most difficult on the mountain. He was glad now that he had followed her.

He continued to look worriedly at the girl, and was relieved to see her struggle to consciousness. She would be okay. He couldn't help appreciate what a beauty she was. A Technicolor redhead, he thought, and then wondered if her eyes would be blue or green. Her vivid hair was plaited into a long braid that now lay across her shoulder. Wild strands of hair struggled for release near every twist, trying to bristle their way out of confinement.

Her skin was remarkable—the color of pure cream. He removed a ski glove and ran warm, curious knuckles lightly over her cheek. Chilled satin. Such skin would have the cosmetic industry out of business in no time, he thought. Noticing a cut on her forehead, he touched it carefully; it didn't look serious. He pulled the gloves back on his hands and gave her a slight shake.

He saw her eyelashes flutter and her pink tongue come out to moisten her lips. Michael watched the play of the tongue. The licking motion struck him as oddly erotic. So, too, were the dark lashes and the half-opened eyes. Aware where his thoughts were taking him, he pulled away. She couldn't be more than sixteen. Eighteen tops. Far too young for a thirty-seven-year-old man with a distinct taste for women of experience.

"Wake up. Can you hear me? Wake up," he barked.

Nicole felt strong hands grip her shoulders, shake her. As she came fully awake, she felt cold, as though someone had tucked her in under an icy sheet. She shuddered, shook her head, and forced her eyelids to open. A figure, dimly backlit by the darkening sky, loomed over her. The only warmth in her body was where the two hands held her shoulders. She forced herself to speak and heard her own voice as if from far away.

"What happened?" She closed her eyes tightly for a second, obliging them to clear. She wanted to see who she was talking to. When her gaze focused, she was looking into a pair of unfamiliar, very intense eyes. Worried eyes, she thought.

"You took a fall, but I don't think anything is broken. Do you feel any pain?" the man asked.

Nicole shifted her body slightly, moved both legs, and wiggled her toes. She sighed with relief. A few aches and pains but no broken bones.

"No, I think everything is all in one piece. Can you give me a hand up? I'm sure I'll be fine."

His eyes looked troubled. "You're sure? That was a pretty tough tumble. You might be suffering from shock."

"I'm okay . . . really." She reached out to him.

His arms were powerful, but it was the gentleness Nicole was conscious of as he lifted her carefully to her feet.

She was instantly dizzy. As she fought for her balance, she fell against his chest and a sharp pain arced through her head, followed by a sudden wave of nausea. She was dimly aware that he was still holding her up. Now both arms circled her. There was comfort in the arms, and their steadiness eased the pain in her head.

"Well?" he asked.

"Well, what?" Nikki's voice was a barely audible murmur.

"Are you going to be okay, or are you going to lean on me for the rest of the night?" She felt rather than saw him smile. "Not that I mind, you understand," he finished in what sounded to Nikki like a lame attempt to be sympathetic.

Nikki realized she was clinging to him and quickly moved from the warm circle of his arms. Nikki Johnson didn't lean on anybody! With the movement, the pain in her head thundered back. She resolved to ignore it.

"Are you sure you're okay? You don't hurt anywhere?" he asked again.

She looked up to dark-green eyes boring into hers as if on a truth-seeking mission. The pain in her head momentarily forgotten, Nikki was struck by their unusual shade. The color of cedar boughs, she decided, with a glint of gold.

"A bit of a headache. Nothing serious. I need a minute to catch my breath and I'll be fine." She tried a smile.

Even through the pain in her head, she could see her rescuer was a ruinously attractive man. She made note of the even white teeth and solid jaw, the slight but sensuous fullness of his lower lip. His face was angular, framed by straight ebony hair that grazed the collar of his ski jacket. Nikki guessed the hair was unruly. He wore no hat, she noticed, only a headband. Amber goggles rested above it. There was something vaguely out of place about him, a certain male elegance uncommon on the West Coast. Maybe it was the cut, the style, of his ski clothes. European, she concluded, definitely not local. There was a hint of an accent, too, although she couldn't place it.

He seemed unaware of her scrutiny when he spoke. *He's probably accustomed to it,* she thought, and pulled her eyes away.

"You should have got off at midstation like I told you. You're not experienced enough to take on this mountain. Particularly in these conditions. If you'd taken the time to read the signs, you would have seen that Cougar Chute is for experts only."

The condescension in the tone brought a crashing end to her flattering appraisal and instantly galled her. He might be a handsome devil, but he was certainly short in the charm department, she decided. Being put down by a total stranger wasn't high on her list of favorite pastimes. Besides, she was an excellent skier, had even done some downhill racing in Colorado. Just who the hell did he think he was anyway?

Her response was curt. "Look, thanks for your help. I appreciate it, but I think I can manage from here."

In truth, she wasn't sure she could manage at all. Her head was pounding, the nausea persisted, and it was a long way to base and the shelter of the chalet. She'd make it, though, and she'd make it without any more help from this know-it-all stranger.

As she bent to pick up her poles and step into her skis, her aching head protested. Her hand automatically went to the offending temple, giving it a light rub. She winced as she did so.

"Let me see that," he demanded.

He lifted her hand from her forehead, then removed his glove. The fading light made him move closer. He examined the damaged skin with a light touch, stroking her brow softly before moving his cautious fingers upward to her hairline. His probing fingers found their target.

"Ouch!"

Quickly, he pulled his hand away. "I thought so. You have the start of a nasty goose egg, little lady. Your wipeout has drawn a bit of blood. Fortunately, the cold is slowing its flow. You may even have a slight concussion, though I doubt it. We should get moving. Do you think you can make it to the next station?"

Even through the pain in her head, Nikki was annoyed. It had been a while since anyone referred to her as "little lady" in quite that tone of voice. She was twenty-seven years old, for heaven's sake, a sales manager for a now-international company. Maybe she looked young for her age, particularly in ski gear, but she didn't look juvenile enough to be taken charge of by a man not more than thirty-five at the outside. *I'm grateful for his help*, she thought, *but not grateful enough to play the helpless female for one more moment.*

"Look . . ." Nikki began, her voice a half octave lower and as frigid as the mountain they stood on.

"Mic—" He started to introduce himself.

She was quick to interrupt. "I'm not interested in knowing your name or anything else about you. I'm interested in you accepting my thanks for your help and leaving me to go on my way. I can make it on my own from here." Nikki crunched her ski poles solidly into the frozen snow and looked around for her hat.

"Not a chance. I'll ski with you to get some help. I want to be sure that cut is looked at. As for you being capable of making it on your own, that's open for debate. You haven't done too well so far, I've noticed. I'm not about to ski off into the night only to wake tomorrow to news that a girl was found frozen four thousand feet up this mountain."

Nikki swung about to look at him. The hard set of his jaw told her arguing would be pointless. Great!

"Fine. Suit yourself," she said. She'd just have to outski him. She had no intention of stopping for first aid. She had work to do.

She spotted her missing toque and bent to retrieve it. The act brought another surge of nausea. A quick shake and the hat was on her head, drawn down to fit closely over her chilled ears. She felt his eyes on her and looked up. His mouth twisted into a grin. He looked first at her and then to the top of her head.

"Interesting hat," he said.

For a fraction of a second, Nikki felt foolish. She'd forgotten how ludicrous the hat looked, but she wasn't about to explain.

"I like it," she replied, lifting her chin.

She shoved off and rapidly gained speed. She glanced back to enjoy the surprise on his face. Caught off guard, he pushed himself to catch up. In seconds, they were skiing side by side down the broad white mountain.

As they approached the next station, Nikki's head felt like it was going to explode, but she was determined to stick to her plan and go for the base.

To her chagrin, he was keeping up with her. He was one hell of a skier. It would be easier if he weren't. If she was to leave him behind, she had to increase her speed.

Nicole drove herself to pass him, and succeeded long enough to fly by the station. She might make it yet. As if reading her mind, the man skiing at her side increased his own speed and was soon in front of her.

He skied back and forth in her path, forcing her to slow down. Nikki saw it was useless, turned her skis, and pulled to a stop. He was directly in front of her, and she was livid.

"That's better." He spoke with irritating self-assurance. "You're one stubborn little lady, aren't you? Did you seriously propose to ski all the way to base after a fall like that? I'm sure the ski patrol has better things to do than go out in the dark to find an irresponsible skier unconscious in a snowbank. A skier who's obviously skied enough to know better."

While she welcomed his reappraisal of her skiing ability, she was enraged by his calm, take-control attitude. The "little lady" bit was driving her crazy.

From her time working ski patrol in Colorado, she knew he was right. There were many occasions when her patrol went out searching for skiers who didn't take the proper precautions for their personal safety. At best, they were an inconvenience, and at worst, a serious threat to the safety of others, often requiring help after dark and in dangerous weather.

The sudden stop made her nauseous again. Yes, she knew he was right, but still she bristled. She'd had enough of his sarcasm, superiority, and condescending demands. She wanted him gone. Period.

"Would you please go wherever it is you were going before you decided to manage my life and let me look after myself. If it makes you feel any better, I'll go in, get some first aid, and ask for some help down. Okay? Now go, just go. Will you?"

His response was swift. "No."

"*No?* For heaven's sake, why not?" she replied in total exasperation. "Isn't that what you were *demanding* I do just moments ago?"

With a quick snap, he raised his ski goggles over his forehead and glared at her. "Because I don't trust you. That's why, and because, Miss High Speed Downhiller, we're already well past the station, and I don't think you're capable of the hike uphill. I know damn well *I'm* not. You've already cost me the last run of the day. The only damn run I've been able to fit into this bloody weekend, and I have no intention of being dragged further into your personal masochistic marathon."

He used a ski pole to point to the ski run they'd just come down. When he spoke, his tone softened slightly. "Look at that slope. Be reasonable. There's no point in going backward."

This was the most infuriating man she had ever met! Why wouldn't he go? Nikki glanced angrily back up the mountain and bit on her lower lip. They'd covered more ground than she'd thought. With her aching head and untrustworthy stomach, hiking back up would be torture. Her frustration was total as she considered her options and shivered. Without the movement of skiing, the cold crept over her skin like a frigid rash. She felt worse by the minute. Like it or not, she couldn't stand here, she decided, but was damned if she'd admit defeat to this pompous bully. Anger again charred her words.

"Maybe you can't make it, but I can. You might also consider that the choices at the moment are limited. Up or down. That's it. If I choose up, that's my business, and I don't need a pigheaded, arrogant, self-important egotist like you telling me what I can and can't do. Now please leave me alone—or to be even more direct, *Get lost!*"

Nikki's voice raised and she could feel her control slipping. The anger and the strain of fighting back tears of exhaustion was more than she could handle. With hostile, pain-filled eyes, she directed a defiant glance at her tall companion, whose look of frustration exactly matched her own, kicked off her skis, and started to climb.

Within two steps, she fell facedown in the snow, its icy top layer abrading her delicate skin like sandpaper. Her sense of aggravation grew. Tears stormed her eyelids, but she didn't give an inch. *Put one foot in front of the other*, she told herself, *that's all it will take*. She did not look back.

THREE

Michael stood silently, debating whether or not to let her go. She was a prickly little thing, and damned if she hadn't made it plain his help wasn't wanted. He should let her go her own way. She wasn't seriously hurt, judging from the way she'd hot-dogged down the mountain. Still, he was curiously reluctant to let her out of his sight. Why?

Was it because of the powerful reaction he'd had moments ago when he held her against him? He was a little disgusted with himself. She was just a kid, but a kid in a woman's body. The primal male in him was certain of that. Maybe, he mused, she was older than she looked. *Or maybe, Michael Patrick Dorado, you've been too long without a woman.*

The unexpected surge of passion had caught him off guard, frustrated him. When he started to wonder how her body would feel pressed against his without the wall of heavy ski togs, he told himself to cool down. *You've got better things to do this weekend than take up after ski bunnies,* he admonished himself, then added, *very young bunnies.*

He watched her stubborn effort to clamber up the slope. The snow, deep and with a fine layer of ice on its surface, impeded her every step. She floundered but didn't quit. His mouth twisted to resist a grin. She was plucky, he'd grant her that.

Maybe he was too rough on her, issuing instructions like a Dutch uncle. Too many planes, too many business meetings, and too long in the office, he decided, with everyone looking to him for decisions. He hadn't bargained on so much desk time when he took over Prisma after his mother's death.

The company was a constant reminder of her. It was her passion, the foundation of his fortune, and now a demanding legacy. More like a leg iron, he thought.

He was anxious to find a new president and pass on the reins of power. He knew Darlene Nichols wanted it—badly. Probably believed she'd earned it, working so closely with his mother for so many years. But he knew she lacked the creativity, the special magic needed to make a business grow and prosper. A magic Megan O'Shea Dorado had in abundance.

Even as his thoughts rambled, Michael kept his eyes fixed on the copper-haired girl in the scarlet toque, still uncertain about the wisdom of leaving her on her own. He measured her progress. She'd made little headway since her first faltering step, and when her next one sent her tumbling backward, he unhesitatingly moved toward her.

Lifting her by her shoulders, he spun her around and pulled her close. When she started to object, he held her from him and placed two fingers, still encased in a leather ski glove, gently on her protesting mouth.

"Will you *please* listen to me?" he asked.

Exhausted, she stared up at him.

His green eyes glittered in the failing light, and a delicate sifting of snow burnished his lashes. His mouth brushed her forehead as he pulled her to the heat of his chest.

Nikki could feel his lips moving against her hair as he spoke. His voice was warm, its pitch lower as he soothed and comforted her. "I'm not trying to bully you, just look out for you. Whether you realize it or not, you're hurt and you're tired. Will you let me decide what's best? Just this once?"

Still with his hands on her shoulders, he held her from him and looked once more into the cloudy blue of her eyes. His question was direct. "Come with me?"

His soft voice and concerned look unsettled her. She was finding it more and more difficult to beat back the sickness and exhaustion caused by her uphill trek. Like a ship in rough water, she was drawn to a safe harbor.

"Where?" was all the answer she could manage. She knew when she was beaten, but her pride demanded he not see it.

She pulled away from him and instantly regretted it. Wrapping her arms across her chest, she rubbed at them in a vain effort to simulate his warmth. She was freezing.

"I have a cabin not too far from here. You can rest a while, and I can repair the damage done to your pretty head." His eyes, shaded by evening cloud, kept their hold on her. "Doesn't that sound reasonable, under the circumstances? Isn't it easier to ski—slowly—downhill for a while longer rather than trudge back up?"

Standing, frozen and despondent, in a snowfall growing heavier by the second, and with the ache in her head now taking on a life of its own, she raised her eyes to his and nodded mutely. He hugged her again to give her heat, and his breath warmed her ear when he told her everything would be okay, not to worry.

She wouldn't worry. She would go with this tall stranger. He was strong and he was warm. For now that was all that mattered. *This man would never hurt me,* she told herself, idiotically feeling as though she had known him forever. Besides, there was probably a phone there and she could call Amy, let her know she was okay. By now she would be starting to worry.

"Was that a yes? Will you come with me?"

Nikki again nodded.

"Good." He bent to retrieve his ski poles and help her put on her skis. "It's not far. Just follow me." He lowered his goggles and headed down the mountain. Nikki followed.

He skied slowly, constantly looking over his shoulder to ensure that she was close behind him. He needn't have worried. Energy spent, Nikki thought of nothing but the warmth and rest promised for the end of this run. No longer able to ignore the sharp pain at her temple or her queasy stomach, she was grateful when she heard him say, "Take it easy now. We're almost there."

Take it easy, she thought. *That's a laugh. I couldn't move faster if I wanted to.* She craved sleep and could not remember ever experiencing such bone-melting fatigue. *I only hope we get there before I'm forced to a complete stop.*

The hope was realized seconds later when Nikki followed him through a stand of trees. The snow was falling in earnest as they reached their destination.

"This is it. I told you it wasn't far. The mudroom is on the right. Follow me," he said.

Nikki kicked off her skis, now so tired that the small task was a supreme effort. Awkwardly, she bent to pick them up and was grateful when he got to them first. He deftly organized both pairs and easily carried them under one arm. Offering his free hand to her, he helped her up the incline at the side of the house.

Even through her pain and the cold, Nikki could see

that using the word cabin to describe this place was understatement. Constructed of stone and log, the house was magnificent, with a towering roof line rivaling the mountains themselves. A prow-shaped front with floor-to-ceiling glass offered a vista of valley and white-cowled mountains. To the left, she could see the soft glitter of Whistler Village now barely visible through the snow and fading light.

They entered on the lower level into an area set aside for skis and other paraphernalia associated with the sport. Nikki watched vacantly as he stowed the skis and removed his jacket. She admired the way he moved—surely, deliberately, nothing wasted or clumsy. He turned to her with that same deliberateness.

"You okay?"

She nodded, but she was anything but okay. She felt peculiar, as though she were in a trance, vision clear but senses blunted and dull. She was sitting on a long pine bench. As if in slow motion, she bent down to take off her boots.

"Here, I'll do that. You sit back and try to relax."

She didn't object, but watched silently as his hands brushed hers aside. When he undid the buckles and removed the cumbersome boots and heavy ski socks, she wiggled her toes and sighed. He'd taken charge again, but she didn't mind. Didn't mind at all. He started to rub warmth back into her frozen feet, and she leaned back gratefully.

Slowly, he massaged each foot in turn, flexing and pulling, rubbing gently, then briskly, then gently again. He didn't once raise his dark head as he continued the rhythmic massage. Stroking, rubbing, kneading the heat into the cold flesh of her feet. Without warning, the warmth turned to fire. Nikki's breath quickened, and she became acutely aware of his expert touch. His two hands, like hot flints, now burned. When his fingers shifted upward to rub and flex her ankle, she yanked her foot from his hands and pulled the other from his knee where he had rested it. Childlike, she tucked them both safely under the bench, crossed, and out of harm's way.

"That's fine. Thanks," she mumbled when he looked up at her.

For the first time in their uneasy relationship, he smiled. The hint of a crease emerged on his left cheek, and one dark brow arched as the smile deepened. Nikki took a breath, then forgot to exhale. The smile was pure seduction. This man was devilish, she concluded. She suspected he knew exactly what he was doing with his blasted foot massage—and the effect it had on her. There was no remorse in the smile, only the broad hint of a tease, its openness attracting her in a way she wished it wouldn't. Her eyes followed the curve of his mouth; his firm, clearly defined lips were now in a questioning grin. She was staring.

"Is something wrong?" he asked, interrupting what was fast becoming an in-depth examination of his face.

She blinked. What on earth was the matter with her? He must think she was an idiot. A pale red stain moved up her neck. She didn't answer, but she did manage to let her breath out.

"Feel better, or is there something else I can do?" His tone was both knowing and sympathetic. Again the arched eyebrow, black as a raven wing. *He's patronizing me,* she thought. *The poor little girl who can't control her eyes.* She was mortified.

"No. Nothing. Thanks." She worked to cool the blush in her cheeks. "Sorry to be such a nuisance. I feel like the village idiot. I haven't taken a spill like that in years. I should be at the base of the mountain by now. Not at the mercy of a stranger in a strange house."

"Somehow I can't quite see you at the mercy of anyone." He grinned. "Although I admit the idea has some tantalizing aspects. But you can rest easy. I'm not in the habit of taking advantage of young girls. As for the stranger part, you can call me Mike. Okay? Come on upstairs. If we're lucky, there might be some hot chocolate for you and an Irish coffee for me." He took her hand, helped her to her feet, and pulled her toward the stairs.

Hot chocolate! Was this guy for real? The grating irritation returned in full measure. Why did he persist in referring to her as young with a capital Y? With the next breath, Nikki grudgingly admitted it wasn't his fault. Everyone made the same mistake. Sometimes she wondered if she was the only woman of her age in the world with the task of forever explaining she was eight or ten years older than she looked.

As they climbed the stairs to the main part of the house, she considered telling him she wasn't as young as she looked, but thought better of it. If he thought she was only a kid, all the better.

"Are you planning on wearing that hat all night? Fetching as it is, you might find it a bit warm." He tossed her a quick smile and then busied himself at the fireplace, crumpling newspaper, adding kindling, then a large log.

The damn hat! She had pulled it above her ears when they came inside but forgot to take it off. She must look a sight with the silly thing perched on her head like a stuffed parrot. She whisked it from her head and stood uncertainly watching him build the fire. She was beginning to feel strange again. It must be the heat. *Stuporous, that's how I feel,* she decided. *That's it exactly.*

"Why don't you sit down before you fall down." He motioned toward the sofa.

"Thanks." She sank into an oversize corduroy chair near the fireplace and rested her head on its high, soft back. Her eyes closed, and she worked against the fatigue that threatened to overwhelm her. She concentrated on the headache. Less violent now, but still persistent. It lurked in the back of her skull and she knew any swift movement would yank it forward.

Carefully, she sat up and looked to her host, who was poking at the beginnings of flame in the fireplace. As she did so, a drop of blood fell on the knee of her ski suit. "Do you have any aspirin and . . . maybe a bandage?" she asked.

How strangely weak she felt. Almost faint. She raised a hand to her forehead in an attempt to stop any blood from staining her or the furniture.

Mike jumped to his feet and crossed to where she was sitting. "Here, get out of that chair and move over here." He helped her take the few steps to the sofa. When she was lying down, he found a pillow for her head. "There. Lie quietly for a minute, and I'll find something for that cut and the headache."

In seconds, he was back. Putting one hand behind her neck, he lifted her head enough for her to swallow some aspirin and take a couple of sips of water. He let her head down gently.

"Thanks. I should be all right in a minute or two," she said.

"Sure you will. I'll put some antiseptic on the cut and a cold compress on the swelling." He grinned at her. "After that you should be ready for another downhill run."

He stroked the hair back off her forehead with cool efficiency, applied antiseptic to the wound, and covered it with a bandage. When the antiseptic stung, she winced slightly.

"Sorry. Did I hurt you? I'm not in my element here.

Playing nursemaid is out of my line." He finished by laying a damp towel over her forehead. "How do you feel?"

His hand continued to exert gentle pressure on the compress as he looked at her.

"Better every minute." She liked him being close to her. She liked looking into those green eyes. Green for go, she thought idly.

"Can I get you anything else? What about that hot chocolate?" He removed his hand from the compress and Nikki instantly abandoned her musings.

"I'd like to use your phone."

"Don't have one."

"You don't have a phone?" She looked around the luxurious log home incredulously. "You're kidding!"

"No phone. At least not here. If there is someone you want me to call—perhaps your parents—I can walk to the neighbors. It's not far from here."

"This is incredible. How can you not have a phone? Everybody has a phone." Nikki, like most people who worked in sales, lived her life with a phone to her ear. She could not imagine being without one.

"This place belongs to a lawyer friend of mine. My guess is he comes here to get away from the damn thing," he explained patiently. "Now do you want me to make that call or not?"

"I'll make it myself." Nikki started to sit up but was quickly restrained by his strong hand on her arm.

"I don't think that's such a good idea. You, little lady, need a rest. Give that cut a chance to stop bleeding and the bump on your head to go down. I'll make the necessary calls. Just give me the number."

"How do I know you will?" Nikki was once more suspicious. "How do I know you'll call anybody?"

The question seemed to puzzle him. Then he laughed outright, and she felt foolish.

"You don't trust me, do you? What are you thinking? That I will only pretend to make your call then come back here and spend the night ravishing you? You've got a vivid imagination, young lady." He looked insulted.

"Is it such a strange thought, given the circumstances I find myself in?" she challenged.

He had moved to stand by the fireplace and no longer prevented Nikki from sitting up. She held the cool towel to her head and sat up very slowly.

"No. I suppose not so strange, considering the times we live in. Though I hope you'll learn to become a better judge of character as the years go on. I'll say it again. I have no evil designs on you. I prefer the company of *women*. The grown-up kind. My only concern is to see you delivered to your family in one piece. That done, I will happily remove myself from your young life—and Technicolor daydreams. What I am *not* doing is letting you go out in the cold and trudge through the snow to make a phone call. That, as they say, is final. Now give me the telephone number and I'll make your call."

The arrogance of the man! Lulled into a sense of well-being by the soothing compress, she leaped angrily to her feet.

"Just who do you think you are. If I say I'll make my own call, I'll—" The reaction of her poor head to the abrupt change in position was thunderous. The headache roared back; so, too, did the queasiness in her stomach. Hands clutched to her middle, she looked up at him.

He did not move from his place near the fire. "I rest my case" was his only comment.

"Where's the bathroom?" was hers.

FOUR

Michael walked back from making Nikki's call. His shoulders and bare head were swathed in snow, but he didn't bother shaking it off, wasn't even conscious of it. Nicole Johnson. It was a name he was familiar with, thanks to Jayne Kingway. What was it she called her? Kingway's rising star.

His surprise when she'd asked him to call Amy Thurston at Chateau Whistler had gone unnoticed by his sickly houseguest. Given in a rush, as she hied her upset stomach to the bathroom, there was no time for him to let her know he knew Amy. It was painfully obvious that the trip to the bathroom took priority.

Nicole Johnson, he said again. It wasn't exactly how he planned to meet her. He chuckled. He guessed it wasn't how she planned to meet him, either—trading insults on a ski run. It was awkward for both of them. He was glad to discover the appealing woman at the cabin was well past the age of consent, but disappointed to find out she worked for him.

It was his rule—and he'd never broken it. No romantic relationships with employees. In honesty, the rule was yet to be tested. He'd certainly never had to apply it to a willful redhead, with eyes as blue and steady as the water in Bantry Bay on a calm summer's day. And he wasn't at all sure he wanted to.

Nikki had returned to the sofa shortly after Michael left to make her call. She'd fallen asleep instantly and was still sleeping when he returned. It was only when he pulled a blanket over her that she stirred.

"What time is it?" she asked groggily.

Michael, fearing to wake her completely, didn't answer. He moved silently from the room and closed the door, going back only once in the next hour to stoke the fire.

For a time, he stood over her, studying her face, now lit only by the dancing flames in the fireplace. The soft light played across delicate skin, shadowed by the sweep of her lashes and the loose tendrils of hair at her temple. The bandage, he could see, showed a slight stain, and her long braid had lost its symmetry, curving around her throat like a wide, shimmering ribbon. Her red hair intrigued him, and he thought of freeing it completely and running his fingers through and down its length.

Nikki shifted to the comfort of her back. Raising one arm, she used it to cradle her head. The blanket shifted downward with the movement, exposing the top portion of the long zipper on her jumpsuit. Opened a mere six inches, it exposed only the vaguest beginning of her curves, but the promise was evident as the form-fitting suit pulled tightly across her breasts.

Momentarily transfixed by the glint of the zipper, Michael wondered what was below that silver strand. Seeking safer territory, his eyes moved back to the oval of her face, then rested on her loosely parted lips. He took a deep breath. With this woman, he knew there was no safe territory. He was aroused just looking at her.

Damn the fire in your Spanish blood, Michael Patrick Dorado, he thought, and the Irish romanticism that fuels it!

He left the room.

It was ten o'clock when he returned to his sleeping beauty. He placed a hand on her shoulder.

"Nikki, wake up." It was the first time he spoke her name.

Nikki responded with a feline stretch. The ski suit again pulled tight across her breasts. Michael swore under his breath. He didn't need a reminder of what he had struggled to forget for the past two hours. He moved to the safety of the fireplace and waited for her eyes to open. There were times when being a gentleman was pure hell.

He'd decided to forego explanations of who he was and what he had discovered during his call to Amy. It would only create an awkward situation for both of them, and tomorrow was soon enough for that. Another long look at the beguiling woman on his sofa affirmed his decision. Keep it light, keep it friendly, and get her out of here—fast, before he did something good little boys, and ethical bosses, didn't do. That was the wise thing to do. *Not that you've always been wise when it comes to women,* he reminded himself.

Nikki opened her eyes. There was only a moment's disorientation in her quick mind before she recalled the events of the past few hours and remembered where she was. She sat upright and was pleased to find her headache was gone. She raised her eyes to her host, and the intensity in his eyes disconcerted her.

"I can't believe I slept so long. Why didn't you

wake me?'' Self-consciously, she pulled the long braid forward and made a halfhearted effort to tidy it.

"I considered it," he replied, "but I thought you needed the sleep. It's the best way to get rid of a headache. Better?" His dark eyes scrutinized her. There was a strange intimacy about the look.

"Much better. Thanks."

When her host continued to gaze down at her, she suddenly felt shy, awkward. Her hand nervously pushed at her hair. There was a subtle change in him, she noticed, again glancing up at him. He didn't seem quite the same as he was before she went to sleep, but she couldn't say what was different. The silence was disturbing; Nikki ended it.

"Did you manage to reach my friend Amy?"

"Yes, I did. I told her you were okay and that I'd bring you home later tonight. She was very relieved." He didn't elaborate.

The room was in shadow, lit only by the fire. Nikki watched as Michael came toward her, his movement fluid and purposeful. He knelt at her feet and reached up to the lamp on the table to her left. As he switched it on and reached toward her face with his right hand, Nikki's eyes widened, and she recoiled as though he would strike her. Her heart beat within her like a thing caged. He hesitated briefly before lightly touching the soiled bandage on her forehead. His eyes moved down from the wound to hers. Confused by her odd response, Nikki looked for reassurance in his emerald eyes now only inches from hers. She found none. It was desire that glittered there. It was in his eyes but not his voice when he spoke again.

"Some blood has seeped through your bandage. I think I should change it. I'll get a fresh dressing."

Nikki seized the moments alone to try to make sense out of her truant emotions. Why these strange reactions to this man? Her logical mind looked for reasons. She was tired, addled from the fall, ill at ease being in a strange house. True, but it didn't account for the peculiar shyness that came over her when he gave her the simplest of attentions. Shy. She was never shy.

She tried to find a label, a recognizable tag for the emotion he evoked in her. It eluded her. *What's the matter with me?* she thought. She answered her own question. *You are avoiding the obvious, Nicole Johnson. He excites you. You're attracted to him.* She argued the point. *It couldn't be that simple. I've been attracted to men before, but I've never felt what I'm feeling now, almost afraid, like I'm at the start of an unknown road with no signpost. But you've never met a man like* this one, *and you know it. This, Nicole,* she said to herself, *is* not *a problem. Travel the road a while. See where it leads. You are, after all, young, healthy and well over twenty-one.*

She was interrupted by his return.

"This should do it, I think." He put bandage and antiseptic on the table. His hand again moved to her forehead. This time Nikki didn't flinch.

"Ready?" he asked, and simultaneously gave a sharp tug on the soiled bandage. She barely felt it.

Michael looked at the exposed wound. "It's not a cut as much as an abrasion. It should heal without a scar." He applied the bandage deftly and was on his feet. He seemed anxious to put distance between them. "That should be the last of my clumsy ministrations. I hope I didn't hurt you." His smile was questioning.

"No. Not at all. Your touch is very . . . gentle." Her fidgety hand stroked the new bandage.

Nikki didn't like the use of the word *last*. Only a few hours ago she'd wanted to rid herself of this man. Now she wanted anything but. *Fool,* she shouted inwardly. *You're acting as old as the teenager he thinks*

you are, and quickly developing a schoolgirl's crush.
Somehow it was important to set him straight. But
how?

It was then she remembered. He'd called her Nikki.

"How did you know my name? You called me by
name when you woke me up."

"Your friend Amy told me. I was already at the
phone when I realized I had no idea who you were. I
described you by telling her that I had come into possession of a red-haired girl with a strange taste in ski
hats." He grinned.

His grin was infectious; she smiled back. Still, she
owed one to Amy for the hat.

"It is distinctive, isn't it?"

"Maybe even a lifesaver. If it wasn't for that hat,
you might still be facedown in a snowbank. When I
saw those neon pompoms disappear down Cougar
Chute, I decided to follow. Without it, I might not have
found you. We might never have met."

"That would have been—" She stopped, not knowing exactly what to say.

"A great loss," he finished. "A terribly great loss."
His smile faded, but his eyes gleamed in the firelight.

Nikki's mouth went dry. So, too, did her meager
store of small talk. The demand now was for substance.
Was the room vibrating or was that her overactive
imagination? She swallowed. Did this man, this Mike,
have any idea the effect he was having on her? She
dropped her eyes, took a breath, and forged ahead.

"You called me a girl. I'm not exactly a girl, you
know." It was more of a stammer than a statement.

"I know." He said no more.

Nice try, Nikki, she said to herself. *A truly top-
drawer effort. He's so excited by that flash he can
barely contain himself.*

"I think I'd better be going." She rose unsteadily

from the sofa. This time it was not nausea or a head-ache that made her legs untrustworthy. She kept her eyes averted. "Can you call me a taxi?" As she said the words, Nikki remembered and her eyes looked to him in confusion. "Oh. I forgot. No phone."

"I'll drive you, but don't you think you should eat first? I'm sure I can rummage something up. Don't expect too much, though. My cooking is about on a par with my medical skills."

"No. I think I should go. It's late. I'll get something at the chalet."

"You're sure?" he questioned, one brow lifting as though to punctuate.

"Yes. Sure. You've done enough. But thanks anyway."

"I'll get a jacket and go warm the car then." There was only the briefest hesitation before he again left the room.

Nicole was disappointed when he was so quick to let her go. Immediately she was ashamed of herself and her wild imaginings. *You've ruined the man's entire day and evening*, she said to herself. *It's understand-able that he's anxious to see the back of you. For all you know he had a date tonight. It isn't likely someone who looks that good planned to spend the night alone. Get a grip on yourself, woman. At least manage a gra-cious exit.* She stood up and went to the fireplace.

He came back in the room dressed for the outdoors and carrying a red ski jacket. "Here put this on. It's practically a blizzard out there and damn cold. You're inclined to feel the chill more after what you've gone through." He put the jacket over her shoulders and slid his hands slowly down her arms, giving a soft squeeze.

A caress? She turned to him, the puzzle evident in her blue eyes. There was only inches between them. His eyes told her nothing.

"Ready then?" He stepped away from her.

"Ready."

It was cold outside, and Nicole was glad for the added protection of the jacket. The snowfall, caught by a light, gusty wind, swirled around them as they headed for the car. With his hand on her elbow, he helped her up and into the large, four-wheel-drive vehicle. When they were under way, she turned to face him.

"You haven't asked me where I'm staying."

"I know where you're staying. Chateau Whistler. I called your friend, remember?"

"Of course. I forgot." Nikki lapsed into silence. Only occasionally did she sneak a regretful glance at his handsome profile. What was happening here? In minutes she would be at her hotel, they would say courteous goodbyes, and this day would end. She didn't want that, she realized suddenly. There was something left to be done. An idea filtered through. She examined it. Dare she? Why not? *Why the hell not?* A little courage. That's all that was needed, and she had plenty of that.

"Pull over," she said suddenly.

"What?"

"Pull over . . . please."

Michael pulled to the side of the darkened road and turned to look at the woman beside him. Had the ride made her sick again?

"Are you all right?"

"I'm fine." She was staring out the window, chewing on a now-dampened lower lip as if faced with some fearsome challenge. When she stopped chewing, she turned her steady, purposeful eyes to his, but didn't speak. Her expression was a mixture of wonder and resolve.

Michael's gaze was equally steady. A current passed between them; the air was charged with it. She felt it, too, Michael didn't doubt that. What he didn't know was *how much* she felt. He drew back slightly and tapped a finger on the steering wheel, waiting.

He wasn't unaware of his own sex appeal. In the past, not that he was proud of it now, he wasn't above using that appeal. To have the woman of his choice was a given. Women came easily to Michael Dorado— always had. Too damned easily, he often thought. His cousin, Sean, had told him it was probably the reason he'd never married. *You don't value what you don't have to fight for, Michael, me boy,* Sean had said, exaggerating his thick Irish lilt.

Why this strange hesitancy now? Why did this vivid redhead make him wary? He knew what to do to bring her to his arms. Why didn't he do it? *She works for you, you idiot. That's why. Exercise a little control here. That's all that's required.*

He scanned her pale face, mesmerized by the lift of her chin, wide-set eyes, her moist full lips, pink from her nervous chewing of moments ago. He wanted those lips. God, how he wanted those lips. His insides were knotted, passions coiled in tight but tenuous control. As he waited for her to speak, he could think of nothing but starting the car and getting this temptress home. Almost nothing.

"You may think this a little odd. You might think *I'm* a little odd, but would you mind . . ." She started and stopped. He watched her take a deep breath to inhale resolve. Her gaze strengthened then, and she leveled her shoulders. "Would you mind kissing me?"

He hadn't expected this. He heard the sane voice of reason, hesitated, then reached for her. The tight coil began to unwind. One kiss. One small kiss. What could it hurt? He'd just keep a lid on it, that's all.

Nikki moved into his arms. She could hear his

breathing as he lifted her chin. His eyes, narrowed and questioning, looked into hers.

"Are you sure, Nikki? Kisses have a way of starting things."

Sounds good to me, she thought, but was reserved enough not to say it. Instead, she nodded silently and watched as his dark head lowered to hers. His kiss was light, soft, and promising. A brush of a kiss, all warm breath and tingles. His gentle beginning, like an early-spring sun, roused her slowly. When light became heat, he started to pull away, his breath heavy and uneven.

"No, not yet." Nikki wound her arms tightly around his neck and pulled his head back to hers.

"Nikki, this is—" Michael fought for control.

"Great," Nikki whispered to finish. "Just great."

She heard him groan.

He kissed her then until she was weak from the pleasure of it. She loved his mouth, she decided, the heat and sureness of it. This man knew how to kiss, although she did sense he was holding himself back. She breathed in the scent of him and gave a whispered cry, running curious fingers over the taut cords of his neck and upward through the thickness of his ebony hair.

Lost in sensation, she tried to move closer. Michael moaned softly, and she felt a tremor pass through him as his mouth moved across her feverish cheek, then to her neck. For an instant, he tightened his hold on her, burying his head in the hollow of her throat. Nikki shuddered and he released her, cupped her face in his hand and looked down into her shadowed eyes, the expression in his own indecipherable. He took a deep breath and found his voice.

"Enough?" he asked as though seeking her surrender.

"Enough." Nikki answered, giving him a hazy smile. Enough, she thought, for now. They drove the last distance to the chalet in silence. Nikki hoped he was right and that kisses did indeed *start* things. She could think of nothing she'd like more. Curious, she looked at him. He was staring straight ahead, his eyes fixed on the snowy road. He was frowning.

FIVE

Nikki woke the next morning clutching pieces of a hazy dream. The gleam of green eyes, the firmness of a strong, tender mouth, a male voice smoky with passion—her own body, its ability to feel heightened and intensified. A lazy, sensual drift of a dream that could take her anywhere.

"Damn the invention of the telephone," she hissed as its persistent noise, a harsh cross between a ring and a buzz, made it impossible for her to cling to sleep any longer. She reached for it.

"Your wake-up call, Miss Johnson. It's seven o'clock."

Nicole managed a thank-you and threw herself back on the bed, pulling the covers over her head. Five more minutes, she promised herself, reaching again for the fading dream.

"Double damn!" The phone again.

"Hello."

"Hi, Nikki. You okay?" Concern filled Amy's voice. "I called last night, but there was no answer. What time did you get home?"

"I was snug in bed before midnight, and in answer to your first question, I'm fine. No broken bones, just a scrape on the old noggin." Nikki's hand touched the bandage on her forehead. "And I was so tired by the time I hit this bed, I wouldn't have heard a jackhammer let alone the telephone."

"Well, I'm glad you're okay. I worried until I got that call. If you don't mind me saying it, I told you so. You should never have made that last run."

A pleased smile spread across Nikki's face as memories of her tumble and subsequent rescue swept into her mind.

"Oh, I wouldn't say that, Amy. I think it was worth it. Are we on for breakfast? I'll tell you all about it."

"That's what I called you about . . . breakfast. I've got to pass. Darlene Nichols asked me if I'd help register and check in the late arrivals for the meetings this morning."

"Darlene Nichols?" Nikki recognized the name but couldn't place it.

"Executive assistant to the president of Prisma. Same position I have . . . excuse me, *had* at Kingway. On a much grander scale, of course."

"Right. Her name was on the memo organizing these sessions. What's she like?"

"*Muy elegante,* as they say in Spanish. Regal is probably an appropriate word. Smart, organized, and very attractive. The only thing I've got on her is youth. I'd put her between thirty-five and forty-five. Although she's one of those women you're never sure about. You know. Kind of ageless. Anyway, she asked me to help today, and I didn't want to say no. Besides, it will give me a chance to meet a lot of people. So I guess I won't see you until the first session?"

"Prod my memory. What's the first session?"

Nikki sat up in bed. She could hear the rustle of

paper from Amy's end of the phone. "Sales Policy and Procedure." Amy chuckled. "Doesn't that get your juices going?"

"Yuck! Whose brilliant idea was that?"

"Darlene's, I guess. It does sound a tad dull to kick off a sales meeting, doesn't it?"

"Like organized rain at a picnic. Do you think I'll be missed if I no-show? I can use the time to give a last-minute polish to my presentation. I'm sure I can catch up on Prisma's policy and procedures later."

"I don't see why you should, you never caught up with them at Kingway."

Nikki laughed lightly. Amy was right. Nikki had the true salesperson's aversion to forms, policy, regulations. Paperwork of any kind was last on her list of priorities.

"Very funny. How do you know I won't turn over a new leaf now that I'm working for Prisma?" Nikki joked.

"Ha!" her friend snorted into the phone. "I doubt that. Anyway, there's probably going to be well over a hundred people at the session. I'm sure your absence won't be noticed. If it is, I'll cover for you, and John and Christy will be there." Amy paused before she spoke again. "You know, Nikki, I'm beginning to think Jayne was right when she said we could get lost in a crack at Prisma. It seems awfully big all of a sudden. To think this is only the North American sales operation. The European side is four times the size. It's hard to imagine our small group making much of an impact. There may be a few Kingway careers at risk. It won't be like working for Jayne, that's for sure. There will be a lot of changes." Amy's voice trailed off.

"Changes for the better, if we make them that way." Nikki's tone was upbeat. "Jayne wouldn't have sold out if she didn't believe that, and Prisma wouldn't have bought the company if they didn't value it. The only risk we run is not asserting ourselves—becoming invisible.''

Nikki was determined to make the staff and products of Kingway known and respected in the huge Prisma organization. This afternoon was the beginning. ''All the more reason that I take the time this morning to fine-tune my presentation. Wish me luck?'' she asked.

''You know it.'' Amy replied with enthusiasm. ''Although I'm not sure how much luck you need with the amount of work you've put into it. Besides, you only have the president of Prisma to impress and, knowing you, you've probably done that already. Oh, oh! Here comes Darlene in full float. Gotta go. See you this afternoon.''

A soft click ended the conversation, leaving Nikki wondering what Amy meant about 'already having impressed' Prisma's president. She didn't even know the man.

Nikki dialed room service, ordered orange juice, coffee, and a lightly poached egg, then headed for the shower. When she came out of the steamy bathroom, terry clad with her head wrapped swami-style, breakfast was there. She ate quickly, anxious to get to work.

Seductive green eyes were pushed, time and again, to the back of her busy mind. Nikki willed herself to focus on her speech. Green eyes were for later.

She worked until twelve-thirty, stood, stretched, and headed for the closet. It wasn't enough to *be* good, she had to *look* good, too. For the next half hour, she gave the same scrupulous attention to her appearance that she'd given her speech.

The perfectly cut black suit provided a dramatic contrast to her creamy skin and brilliant hair. To complement it she wore a white high-necked lace blouse and added another puff of lace to the breast pocket. Fine Belgian lace, a gift from Amy.

She wove her coppery hair into a loose braid and swept it upward from the nape of her neck, giving some naturally unruly tendrils freedom to frame her face and neck.

With a grimace, she leaned closer to the mirror and pulled the dried bandage from her forehead. She remembered gentler hands than her own doing the same last night. Very gentle hands. Wonderful hands. She was staring at the mirror. *Some hardheaded businesswoman you are, Nicole Johnson. One of the most important meetings of your life coming up in the next hour and you're mooning over a man, a complete stranger at that.* She shook her head and returned her attention to her damaged forehead.

There was still some swelling but not much. Makeup, and some extra softening of her hair would cover it, she decided. She draped a towel over her shoulders to protect her suit and set to it. *A good time to give my new Prisma cosmetics a try,* she thought.

The camouflage proved adequate. From a safe distance, no one would notice. She stepped into a pair of high-heeled Italian leather shoes. Ridiculously expensive, but worth every penny, she thought, eyeing herself in the full-length mirror.

"You'll have to do, kiddo. I can't think of anything more," she said aloud as she added a pair of gold earrings and smoothed her skirt. Again she looked at her image. "Now for the important part." She closed her eyes.

Nikki blocked all other thoughts from her mind and focused on the coming presentation. Her lips moved soundlessly as she mouthed the opening words of her speech, her concentration total. She imagined the crowd, then herself standing before them. She envisioned her success, then played it back in her mind. This visualization technique, used to bolster confidence and prepare for challenging situations, had always helped her in the past. This time when she closed her eyes, she felt a slow flush rise to her cheeks and a creeping sensuality.

"Curse it!" she muttered, angry that she couldn't control her wayward thoughts. A knock at the door marked the end of her weakened ability to concentrate.

She answered it. "Yes?"

"Parcel for Nicole Johnson." A young man smiled up at her.

"Parcel? Just a minute." Nikki went to her purse for a tip.

"Thank you, ma'am."

I must look old enough if he called me ma'am. She smiled to herself and opened the large manila envelope with its curious bulge. Inside was the atrocious scarlet toque and a brief note.

Nikki. Feeling better today, I hope.

> Mike.

P.S. I look forward to seeing you again (perhaps sooner than you might like?).

Nikki puzzled a bit over the last line, but couldn't help the satisfied smile that played across her face. She couldn't deny the powerful attraction of her charming rescuer. She was anxious to explore it, and by the sound of his note, he was, too. Why not? she thought. It's been a long time, and he is one gorgeous man.

She looked again at her watch; 1:10. Time to go. Her stomach gave a nervous roll as she grabbed her briefcase and headed for the door. With her hand on the doorknob, she hesitated briefly, took a deep breath, then said aloud, "Look out, Prisma, here I come."

* * *

The conference room easily held the large crowd. With time to spare before the meeting, the men and women responsible for selling Prisma Cosmetics in North America milled about aimlessly or huddled in groups. Nikki was scarcely in the room before Amy was at her side.

"Quite the group, isn't it? Nervous?" Amy asked.

"I wasn't . . . at least not until I stepped into this room. Now my stomach feels like a Model T on a back road. I'll be okay, but I'm glad I'm first up. I would be more nervous if I had to wait through other presentations."

"Sorry, but I've got some bad news for you. You're *not* first up. Darlene changed the order because the eastern region V.P. has to take an early plane back tonight. Some unexpected business problem, she said. You're now set for three-fifteen, right after the break for coffee."

"Great," Nikki muttered under her breath. She hated last-minute changes.

"Sorry, Niks," Amy said again.

"It's not your fault, Amy, and it's not a problem—honest. I'll cope. By the way, how did the policy and procedure sessions go this morning? Were they as stimulating as the description of them would lead you to believe?"

"You didn't miss a thing, and you weren't the only one not there. Not by a long shot. My guess is a good portion of the distributors and Prisma staff were on the slopes this morning. I don't think our new president is too pleased with the way things are going. I saw him huddling with Darlene after the session, and he didn't look happy. She's been a tyrant ever since. By the way, what did you think of him?"

"Who?" Nikki asked absently, her attention drawn to a tall, commanding woman bearing down on them.

"Mich—" Amy's eyes followed Nikki's. "That's her. That's Darlene Nichols, female extraordinaire. Get ready."

"You must be Nicole Johnson." A firm, expertly manicured hand reached for hers. "I'm Darlene Nichols."

The hand that took Nikki's displayed a gleaming set of acrylic nails, each tip a dark, blooded red. Prisma Night Flame #68, Nikki guessed. She had studied all the latest Prisma colors. If she was going to work for a company, she was determined to know its products. Darlene's handshake was strong and brief. Amy's description was accurate. She was *very* attractive, possessing the polished, sophisticated look of a woman who understands her own style and maximizes it. Amy left out one adjective: formidable. Nikki guessed that behind Darlene's practiced charm lay the tenacity of a pit bull.

Nikki returned Darlene's orchestrated smile with one she hoped was more sincere.

"Has Amy explained to you about the slight change in plan? I hope it doesn't inconvenience you. We're all looking forward to your presentation." Darlene glanced quickly at her watch, seeming not to care whether Nikki was inconvenienced or not. She went on.

"You *will* stick to your time limit and finish by four-thirty, won't you? We're already late getting started. There's a clock on the speaker's dais. Please refer to it often so you stay on track. Oh, there's Donald Wright now. Excuse me, but I think I'll make sure he heads straight for the head table and doesn't get sidetracked." Again, the red-tipped hand reached for Nikki's. "So nice to meet you, dear."

Nikki again shook the outstretched hand, and a wry smile crossed her face as she answered.

"Nice to meet you." They were her first words since meeting the phenomena that was Darlene Nichols.

The tall woman turned to Amy and adopted a more authoritative tone. "Please take Nicole to the table, Amy. I believe her seat position is at the far left." With that she was gone. Her purposeful walk took her directly to Donald Wright.

At her departure, Nikki and Amy turned to look at each other. Nikki's expression, plus a knowing grin, eliminated the need for words. Amy shrugged, rolled her eyes, and shook her head.

"C'mon, Niks. Let's find your seat. By the way, you look terrific. The suit is perfect."

"Thanks, I'm glad you think so. I've been eating bread and gruel for weeks trying to pay for it."

"Well, I can tell you—it's worth it."

The two women headed for the table. Nikki's position was the farthest from the speaker's podium.

She took her chair and looked out over the room of milling people. They were now looking for places among the rows of chairs in front of the raised speaker's platform. Nikki felt her stomach muscles tense. She wished she didn't have to wait. The hour and a half until her presentation would seem an eternity.

"I'd better take a seat while there are some good ones left." Amy started to leave, turned back, and spoke again. "Knock 'em dead, Niks. Do us proud. Okay?"

"I'll give it my best shot, Amy. See you later."

Nikki's eyes followed Amy through the crowd. She wanted to know where she was sitting in case she needed a friendly face to fix on during her speech. When Amy took her place, Nikki saw she was sitting with John and Christy. Both were turned her way, trying to catch her eye. She smiled and lifted her hand. John gave her a V for Victory sign.

The familiar faces eased her jitters. *I'm prepared,* she told herself. *There's nothing to worry about. No reason not to be in perfect control.* Again she focused on her presentation. She was lost in her own thoughts, when she heard voices coming from behind her. There was a tap on her shoulder. It was Darlene Nichols.

"I'm not sure you've met our president, Nicole. May I introduce Michael Dorado. Michael, this is Nicole Johnson from Kingway."

Nikki looked up into a pair of familiar green eyes and gasped. Someone had sucked the air from her lungs, from the whole room! This wasn't right. It was a cruel joke—a nightmare! This *could not* be him, but it was. There was no way there were *two* men who looked like that. She was speechless.

Michael sensed her disquiet and took it on himself to break the tense silence between them. "Nicole and I have already met, Darlene."

The cool reserve in his voice shocked Nikki. She wished for half of it. His eyes met hers with quiet calm, showing no sign of surprise at seeing her seated at the Prisma head table. None at all. She was baffled. He went on, his voice deep and even, his look straightforward.

"Unfortunately, the circumstances didn't allow for proper introductions. That might be causing Nicole some minor embarrassment." An apologetic smile touched his lips as he offered his hand.

Minor embarrassment! Nikki turned the words over in her head. They were hopelessly inadequate. Try major mortification! She had asked this man, *her boss,* for a kiss with all the finesse of a curious, inept virgin. At the thought of it, a crimson tide surged up her neck and covered her creamy skin. Not even her considerable willpower could slow its course. All she managed was a tortured smile as she took his outstretched hand.

When she didn't speak, he continued. He was still holding her hand. "How are you feeling today? No side effects from the fall, I hope?"

She had to speak. Gone was the quick-thinking, fast-talking Nicole Johnson. In her place was a thick-tongued, stuttering idiot. She took a deep swallow, mustered her composure, and adopted her most busi-nesslike voice. It came out like a raspy croak.

"None. None at all. Thank you." She coughed to steady her voice, then aimed a cool, silvery stare into his smiling eyes. She pulled her hand from his.

"My clumsy efforts at first aid were enough then?" The brows raised in question, and his eyes traveled upward to the line of her hair.

"More than enough. I'm fine. One hundred per-cent." The remarks were staccato as one shaky hand fluttered to her forehead and down again.

She continued to marvel at how unperturbed he was at finding out she was one of his employees. *I guess you learn that kind of control when you become head of an international company,* she thought. She, on the other hand, felt like a penniless imp with her grubby hand caught in the licorice jar. *My new boss, and I made a pass at him,* she groaned. *Way to go, Nikki. Way to go.*

Darlene took in the odd exchange, glancing at both of them with a mixture of curiosity and annoyance. She obviously didn't like what she didn't understand.

"How nice that you've met and how mysterious." She turned her gaze to Michael. "You must tell me all about it later when we have more time. Now I think we should sit down, or this meeting will never get started." Again she looked at the fashionably large watch on her wrist. "Fifteen minutes late! We'd better move along."

Michael shrugged and gave Nicole a parting grin as Darlene took possession of him and propelled him to his place at the long table.

Nikki was thankful they were gone. Thankful her scarlet face would have a chance to regain its natural color. For a moment her chagrin centered on Darlene Nichols. *That woman,* she thought sourly, *reminds me for all the world of the Mad Hatter in* Alice in Wonderland. "I'm late. I'm late for a very important date," she quoted to herself. The joke did nothing to lessen the tension building inside her like a rigid tower. She wondered miserably how she would get through the time until her own presentation.

Her boss, she wailed inwardly. That incredible, tantalizing man was her boss. It was embarrassing, humiliating, and . . . too damned disappointing for words. The fates were indeed cruel. She let out a long painful breath and shook her head.

SIX

I'm a blue ribbon heel, Michael told himself, taking his place at the speaker's table. *I should have fore-warned her—mentioned something in the note when I returned her hat. God, when she recognized me, she looked like I'd struck her.* He'd wanted to apologize right then, but it wasn't the time or place.

He looked back at her. She was pulling her chair closer to the table, her copper hair sparkling under the high overhead light. *It's softer today,* he thought. *Must be those wild little curls around her forehead she's using to hide her cut.* He'd had to stop himself from touching that forehead, that clear, beautiful face. He drew in a breath. *And I thought she was a kid.* Some kid. Even the conservative black suit she was wearing couldn't hide the woman he saw today.

From burnished hair to black silk stockings, she was a stunner. He pulled his eyes away. He hadn't gaped so openly at a woman since he was fifteen.

It was that damned kiss! The kiss changed every-thing, and he blamed himself. *Some rule, Michael, me lad. One look from under those long sexy lashes and your resolve melted like late-spring snow.*

He would speak to her privately during the break, set things straight. Then he would smarten up. If he didn't, his time in the Vancouver office during the next month would be uncomfortable for both of them. He had a business to run, damn it, and from what Jayne Kingway said, this woman could play a large part in it, free him to pursue his own interests. It was imperative that his judgment be clear and unbiased.

From the corner of her eye, Nikki watched Michael take the seat of honor near the speaker's podium. She studied him intently. He looked older today, more imposing and definitely more intimidating. She put that down to knowing who he was. He hadn't intimidated her last night. She started to redden again. That damned kiss! She reached for her briefcase to take out her notes and to divert her attention. It didn't work. Her eyes were more interested in the hunk of man than the sheaf of papers.

His dress was casual—a dark sports jacket and slacks worn with a brilliantly white shirt sans tie. He looked tired, paler than she remembered. He was restless, too, as if he would rather be anywhere other than this meeting room. Still, there was no mistaking his polish and control, his cool sophistication. It was in the cut of the man, she decided, not the cut of the clothes.

Nikki was sure every female eye in the room was fixed on him. *Let them have him*, she decided. *I'm not in the market for an affair with my boss, no matter what he looks like*. But why does he have to look *so bloody good?* she moaned.

She watched him get to his feet and extend his hand to the man at his right, who had just arrived. The movement was fluid and agile. He had the ease of a man accustomed to power and deference. And the seductive magnetism of a cat, a big black green-eyed cat, Nikki decided. Unexpectedly, he turned those eyes to her.

Ragged, shivery little tremors rippled from her heart to her stomach. She turned away and did not look back.

Nikki looked through the crowd for the faces of her coworkers. Both Christy and Amy were staring at Michael, each woman lost in her own fantasy, she was sure. Michael Dorado was perfect fantasy material.

John caught her eye and gave her a friendly nod. Dimly, she became aware that Darlene was standing to introduce David Wright and explain the agenda change. When he rose and started to speak, Nikki tried to give him her full attention.

When the drone that was his speech ended, there was some polite applause, and Darlene called a fifteen minute break. Nikki bolted from her seat and merged with the men and women on the floor. She had no desire to exchange more words with either Darlene or the dashing Michael Dorado.

She caught up with Amy at the coffee-and-juice table.

"Want some?" Amy lifted a silvered coffee urn in Nikki's direction.

"No, thanks. Right now a caffeine rush is the last thing I need. I've had all the jolts I can stand for one day."

"What's the matter? Why is your face that color?"

"What color?" Nikki's hand flew to her cheek.

"Ruddy is good, but beet juice is better, I think. You look like you just ran a marathon." She poured herself some coffee.

"I wish that was it. I'm afraid this ruddiness is a symptom of what could be a case of terminal embarrassment."

"Embarrassment?" Amy gave Nikki her full attention. "How come?"

"You see our new president up there?" Nikki nodded in the direction of the head table.

"I sure do." Amy said as she turned her eyes toward Michael. "Unbelievable, isn't he? Like he just stepped off the cover of *G.Q.* There's not a man in the room who even comes close."

Nikki couldn't decide if the dreamy look in her friend's eyes was real or feigned. She looked back at Michael and sighed. It was real all right. Why should Amy be immune?

"Would you believe that's the *Mike* I met last night?" Nikki's tone was urgent.

Amy's questioning look changed to confusion. She looked at Nikki for all the world like she'd lost her marbles.

"I know." The answer was matter-of-fact.

"What do you mean *you know*?" Nikki was stunned.

"I talked to him on the phone, didn't I? Besides, Michael and I go back a while . . ." Amy hesitated as if not wanting to go on.

It was Nikki's turn to be confused. "Go back a while? You mean you know him? From where, when?"

"From my trip to Europe two years ago. I met him in Ireland." A pink flush heightened Amy's complexion.

"Why didn't you ever say anything? I mean the name Michael Dorado has been bandied around the office for weeks. Ever since Prisma bought us. Why didn't you tell me?"

"Because I didn't know him as Michael Dorado. I knew him as Michael O'Shea. And I sure didn't know he was president of Prisma. Not until yesterday. I found out when we met at the lift base, and we talked a little more when he phoned to tell me he would be bringing you home. That's the first I knew of it." Amy looked uncomfortable.

Nikki stared at Amy as if she were a stranger. *And I thought I knew everything there was to know about her,* she thought. So Michael was the stranger she saw kissing Amy. She didn't want to think about how she felt about that.

"Why did he use another name when you met him in Ireland?" she asked.

"I'm not sure exactly. I met him in a pub in Glengariff. That's in the south of Ireland," she explained. "They call it the Irish Mediterranean because of its special climate. Anyway, he was introduced to me as Michael O'Shea. When I asked him about it last night, he laughed. He said when he's in Ireland he's always Megan O'Shea's boy. Everyone calls him that, he said, and he'd long ago quit trying to change them."

"That's a bit strange, don't you think?"

Amy was oddly defensive. "Strange? I don't think so. Maybe he enjoyed the anonymity. When you have a name as famous as Dorado is in Europe, it doesn't seem so strange."

"I wish you would have told me this morning you knew him. Why didn't you?"

"I didn't get the chance. Besides, it's no big deal. So I know him. It's not as if I know him real well or anything. We met. That's about it." Amy's studied nonchalance was a new posture for her. Nikki knew there was more to the story than she was telling. Then it hit her. Michael Dorado must have known who she was when he kissed her. She had to know for sure.

"Amy, when he called last night, did you explain to him who I was . . . that I worked for him?"

"Sure. Didn't he tell you?"

"No. You might say, we didn't, uh, get around to making the proper introductions," Nikki stammered. There was no time for explanations now.

Amy looked puzzled. "Oh? Well, anyway, he was shocked when I told him you were with Kingway. He said that when you gave him my name to call, he thought you were some teenage relative of mine. Isn't that a hoot? I think he thought I was putting him on when I told him you were Kingway's sales manager and that you were making a presentation today. He said, and I quote, 'You're kidding. That I have to see to believe.' I think he found it quite funny. Though not in a mean kind of way." Again Amy spoke in his defense.

"Funny? What's funny about it?" Nicole worked to keep her voice calm.

"I don't know. What are you so jumpy about anyway? What's going on?"

"Nothing's going on and I'm not jumpy. Look, I'll see you later. I'm going to the ladies' room."

Nikki kept repeating the words over and over like a mantra. *I'll show him, I'll show him, I'll show him.*

Here I am, faced with the most important presentation of my career, so mad I could spit. If he was any kind of a . . . gentleman, she sputtered, *he would have told her what he knew. The entire incident could have been avoided. As it was, he'd let her make an ass of herself. What can you expect from a man who operates under an assumed name? Michael O'Shea, if you please.*

Her earlier impression of him was right after all. He was arrogant, pigheaded, conceited, and self-important. Add to that dishonest, slippery, and manipulative, she thought, and you have the man. If he wasn't her new boss, she would . . . she didn't know what she would do, but it would probably carry a life sentence!

The break was over and Nikki strode back to her seat, ignoring her inner turmoil. She reminded herself that nothing had changed. The Kingway people were still depending on her, and she owed them her best. Besides, didn't a certain sneaky green-eyed male say he'd have to 'see it to believe it' before he'd accept her as a professional? *Well, Mr. Michael Dorado,* she said to herself as she sat down, *you are about to see the presentation of your life*.

Nikki barely heard Darlene when she rose from her chair and began her introduction.

". . . so pleased that Nicole Johnson has agreed to tell us a little something about Kingway—the newest member of the Prisma corporate family. Without delay then, Nicole Johnson." Darlene clapped her hands in Nikki's direction and took her chair.

Nikki stepped forward, removed the cordless microphone from its post on the dais, and walked to the front of the platform. She wanted nothing between her and the audience.

"Ladies and gentlemen. I plan on telling you more than a *little* about Kingway. I'm going to tell you *a lot*. I'm going to tell you about the company, the people, and the products—especially the products. Not because they are the most gentle and beneficial products ever developed for a woman's skin. Not because they are of the highest quality and environmentally friendly, from ingredients to packaging, but because. . . ."

Nicole paused, took a step forward, and let her eyes scan the crowd.

"They are the most exciting products available to women today. And, ladies and gentlemen, excitement *sells*." Again she paused. A teasing smile came to her mouth. She spoke again. "You are interested in products that sell, aren't you?" To a room full of salespeople, it was a siren call. She had their full attention.

Nikki held center stage until after five o'clock. She had informed and entertained for over two hours. She was physically drained but absolutely certain she'd made a strong impression on the vast Prisma organization. She finished speaking at four o'clock, leaving half an hour for questions. What she hadn't foreseen was how many questions there would be. They didn't stop. The crowd was hers—and Kingway's.

Darlene ended it when she stepped to Nikki's side at the front of the platform. "Ladies and gentlemen . . ." She raised her hand. "Enough. I think Nicole's voice is going to give out, not to mention her feet. Shall we let her sit down, give her a round of applause, and call it a day?" Darlene took the microphone and nodded Nikki toward her chair.

The sound from the floor was clamorous. Nikki smiled her thanks. Then, finally, it was over. The crowd, still buzzing, started to move toward the massive doors at the back of the room. Nikki stood and gathered her notes, notes she hadn't referred to once in the past two hours. She started to put them in her briefcase.

"I didn't realize you had such a flair for the stage." His deep voice was taunting.

Nikki felt the adrenaline rush abate; irritation surged to replace it.

"Not for the stage, for Kingway Skin Care. I had a job to do, and I did it." She stuffed paper in her case.

"You did it well, extremely well. I wish all the speeches had been as good—and as interesting. I knew Kingway was a valuable acquisition for Prisma, but I didn't realize how valuable until today."

"Thank you, Mr. Dorado. That's good of you to say." Nikki crammed in the last of her papers and started to leave. His voice stopped her.

"*Mr. Dorado?* I thought we were Nikki and Mike."

Nikki fixed him with a cold blue stare. "We were. For an hour or so. That was before I knew better. I hope my familiarity wasn't too distasteful. Of course, *I* had no idea who you were at the time. Had *I* known, *I* would have acted accordingly."

"Oh? How exactly would you have acted?"

"Professionally," she snapped.

"I never intended to deceive you about who I was, Nikki. I tried to introduce myself on the mountain. You said you weren't interested in knowing my name or anything else about me. Those were your exact words if memory serves me." Nikki colored. He was right, but that didn't excuse him from not telling her later.

She continued to glare at him. As though having won a brief skirmish, he smiled. "As for your familiarity, as you call it, it wasn't distasteful at all. Quite the opposite. It's not often a man gets asked for a kiss, you know. And so charmingly, too. Will you think less of me if I admit to being tempted beyond my ability to refuse?"

Had he moved closer with those last words, or was she imagining it? She wasn't imagining the light in his eyes like the fluttering of gaslight before full flame. She took a step back before responding.

"You're nothing if not direct, are you? There are some men, more sensitive maybe, who wouldn't have brought the subject up. Did it occur to you I would rather forget that, uh . . . incident? I'm sorry if I embarrassed you."

This time he did move closer, his gaze intense, his words whispered. "Nikki, you didn't embarrass me, and it's me who owes the apology, not you. You're right, there are men who wouldn't mention the events of last night, but I can't afford to be one of them. First, because we have to work together while I'm on the West Coast, and second, because I would feel even worse than I do now if I couldn't make you believe I enjoyed the kiss as much as I hope you did. If our circumstances were different, if you didn't work for Prisma—" He caught her widening blue eyes with his own. His gaze swept her face like a caress and there was no mistaking they held regret.

The charm of the apology caught Nikki off guard, as did the sincerity in his eyes. Her chest tightened and she dropped her eyes. *Smarten up, girl,* she told herself. *He's your boss. There will be nothing but trouble if you fall for him. He's not a company benefit.* She chose her next words carefully.

"Maybe it's best to forget the whole thing. As you said, we do have to work together. It will be better if the relationship is strictly business. As for *our* circumstances, they are what they are, an employer-employee relationship."

"True. But Prisma's gain of such a dedicated and talented sales professional seems to be my loss."

Oblivious to the few people still milling around the big room, Michael lifted a hand to Nikki's cheek and stroked it softly with his knuckles. "I am not at all sure such a loss is desirable—or even tolerable. But if you promise not to ask for another kiss, I may, just may, be able to keep my baser instincts under control." Michael's slow smile turned to a wide grin as his hand left her face.

Nikki's skin burned at his touch. *I can't seem to control my body heat around this man,* she thought. Her breath caught in her throat. He was teasing her, and she knew she should be angry. She wasn't. She, too, was beginning to see the humor in the situation. Although with Nikki it came more grudgingly. Still, levity was better than a no-win vendetta with the new president. She did, after all, have her career to consider. He was offering a fresh start. Good sense said, take it. She looked up at him through long, dark lashes with a hesitant smile. She matched her tone to his.

"I'll try, Mr. Dorado. Really try. I would not like to be the tainted woman who sullies your virtue."

He threw his head back and laughed outright. It was a deep laugh that showed not only mirth but relief as if some important threshold was crossed. "What virtue I had is long gone, *Miss Johnson*. So you have no worry on that score, but please call me Michael. One of the nicer aspects of doing business in North America is the informality. Friends?" He offered his hand.

"Friends." Nikki forced a bright, positive smile to her lips and took his outstretched hand. It wasn't a friend she was looking for when she asked for that earth-moving kiss, but it was far and away the best offer she'd had all day. As his strong hand slipped away from her softer one, she felt an eerie sense of loss.

"Nikki, there you are. We've been waiting in the hall. We wanted to let you know how good your presentation was." Amy's voice rose from the floor near the platform. She was with John and Christy.

"You were great. Just great. We were proud of you." John reached for her hand, his hazel eyes brimming with admiration.

"Add my kudos to the foregoing," Christy said. "Fabulous job, Niks. Best presentation so far."

"You're probably the most biased group in the room, but thanks anyway," Nikki joked.

"Maybe so, but you sure as hell were better than that tedious, *with a capital T*, policy and procedure thing this morning." Christy was, as usual, forthright. It didn't matter to her that the president of Prisma was within earshot of her criticism. Christy eyed Michael boldly and a bit too appraisingly for Nikki's taste.

She hoped Michael would take Christy's blunt assessment of Prisma's morning meeting in good grace. She needn't have worried; he was grinning at Christy for all the world like he agreed with her completely. Nikki didn't like that, either. What was the matter with her?

"I don't think you've met our new president." Nikki made the necessary introductions.

When she came to Amy, she stopped and looked at Michael. "I understand you two already know each other." She scanned his face for clues to the relationship but found nothing but a friendly smile.

"Yes, we do. Good to see you again, Amy. We have a few things to catch up on before I leave."

As Michael turned his attention to her, an odd expression crossed Amy's face, as though some darkened memory was awakening to new light. The expression made Nikki uncomfortable. She felt intrusive, as though she'd stumbled beyond a no trespassing sign. God, she thought, this man is like a strike in a bowling alley with the women as the pins.

"Michael, nice to see you." Amy extended her hand. "I'm holding you to that catching-up promise. Didn't you think our Nikki was great?"

"More than great. Perfect." He sent a brilliant smile in Nikki's direction. "Now if you'll all excuse me, I have a meeting before dinner . . . for which," he glanced at his watch, "I'm already late. So before I wreak complete havoc on Darlene's schedule, I'd better run. It was a pleasure to meet all of you."

He turned to Nikki then. "Do you think you could spare some time for me tomorrow? Say about eleven? There's something we should discuss before Monday. I also have product plans I think you'd be interested in and some questions about Kingway. After your presentation, I can't think of anyone better able to answer them."

"Tomorrow at eleven is fine. I'll look forward to it. I have some reports with me—historical data, sales figures, and the like. Would you like me to bring them?"

"No. Just bring yourself. There will be time enough to review statistics back in Vancouver. See you tomorrow then." He turned and was gone.

His request had surprised her, but she hadn't hesitated. She was keenly interested in those product plans, in anything that would affect Kingway and its people. Some time alone with the new president would be enlightening on both fronts. Some time alone with the man would be delightful. She wondered about those baser instincts he'd mentioned. Would they really be so easy to unleash? The way Nikki's thoughts were going, she decided she was the one who needed the leash. *Out of bounds,* she told herself for the millionth time, *the man is way out of bounds.*

"I say we go for a celebratory drink. Niks has paved the way for us with our new employer, and she deserves a toast. All in favor say aye." John was taking the vote.

"The ayes have it," he announced before anyone had a chance to respond. He reached up to help Nikki step from the platform.

"I'm for it," she said, "but let's make the celebration a short one. I feel the need to get into some jeans and a T-shirt." She looked pointedly at her three friends and coworkers and added, "Now that there is no longer any need to impress anyone."

"There she goes again. Planning her escape from the bar before we even get there," Christy said. "When have you ever been in a bar for more than a *short* time? Not that we hold that against you, you understand. Someone in this motley crew has to keep a clear head. Better you than me." Christy laughed, took Nikki's arm, and pulled her toward the door. "You must learn the fine art of partying, Niks. Think about what you're missing."

"I know what I'm missing. A big head and a thick tongue the morning after. No thanks. But, believe it or not, I do feel like celebrating tonight, so I might surprise you and stay until lights out," Nikki teased back.

"Are you ready to carry me to my room and put me to bed if I lose control?"

"Let me be the first to volunteer," John said with mock gravity. "It would be my pleasure to tuck you in." He exaggerated a leer. "And of course you could trust me completely."

"I think there's a better chance the person needing tucking in will be you, Zinnser, not Nikki," Christy responded. "And that will take all three of us."

"Whatever." He smiled and waved a hand in casual surrender. "I'm a flexible man . . . a *very* flexible man."

John was a big man, too, well over the six-foot mark, with tawny hair and a wide, crooked grin. A great favorite with Kingway's customers, he was also a big brother to the predominantly female staff at Kingway.

"C'mon, you guys," Amy piped up then. "Let's not just talk about it, let's do it. We'll be lucky to get a table if we waste any more time. And as for Nikki ever drinking too much, I'll believe that when I see it."

As the four of them headed for the Mallard Bar, Nikki was thinking about Amy's words. *I'll believe it when I see it.* That's what Michael had said.

Her father often used those same words. With Taylor Johnson, it was only results that counted, and Nikki's results were never good enough. There were no E's for effort in the Johnson family, no "good try" or "better luck next time" platitudes. You either succeeded, *brilliantly,* or you failed. "You don't set your goals high enough, Nicole. Look at your brothers, how well they do. They succeed because they aim high. You must learn to do the same." Her aim was never high enough, her accomplishments never quite what they should be. There was always the feeling that she was out by one percent.

Quit moaning, Nikki, she told herself. *You come from*

a hard-working, successful family. You should be proud you were taught to work hard, to try to be, and do, your best always. Trying, that was the word. I'm always trying, but it doesn't get any easier.

Maybe Amy is right, she reflected. *Maybe I am becoming a workaholic. After all, selling skin care products is hardly brain surgery. I should relax more, make time for some fun and games.* Nothing too serious, of course, not right now, when there was so much to do. Just a few innocent dates. A little candlelight and wine wouldn't hurt, would it?

Love and romance. How long had it been? She hated the answer. Never. *I've never, ever really been in love,* she admitted, feeling inordinately sorry for herself, *not in all my twenty-seven years.* Wait. There was that one semiserious affair during college, but Dad hadn't approved. "Not an impressive choice, Nicole." That's what he'd said. He was right. When wasn't he right?

Love and romance, she thought again. *Why think of it now when I have the world on my doorstep, a chance for real success?* She knew why. Michael Dorado. Six feet of male flesh put together in a way to tempt any father's daughter, and a kiss that tested the limits of the Richter scale. Why did he have to be her boss? In her mind, the question was followed by three exclamation points and about fifteen question marks.

"Why so thoughtful?" Amy whispered as they took their seats. "You don't want to be here, do you? I know you hate sitting in bars, but try and bear up. John and Christy do want to celebrate."

"It's not that. Just a little postpresentation let-down, I guess. And I do want to celebrate. It's exactly what I need tonight." *What I don't need,* she thought, *is to sit in my room and moon over some globe-trotting, world-weary man who operates under fictitious names. Besides, it's decided—we're to be friends.* The word stung like a wasp bite.

SEVEN

Leaving the bar, Nikki followed the happy threesome into the elevator. She was looking forward to a few minutes alone in her room, and by the sound of it, a few minutes was all she was going to get.

"You're not going to let me beg off then?" she asked.

"Absolutely not. Go to your room, get into those jeans you've been pining for, then meet us in the lobby in, say, twenty minutes. We'll have an early dinner then reconnoiter all available night life." John was adamant. "By tomorrow morning, we'll be fortified enough, or exhausted enough, to withstand another day of Darlene Nichol's seminars. Then it's homeward bound."

"You're sure jeans will be okay?" Nikki asked.

"As long as you haven't been changing the oil in your car in them, they'll be fine. This is Whistler, remember, and so far they haven't passed any laws to prohibit comfort."

"All right, you win, but it will be closer to thirty minutes. I'm going to grab a quick shower."

"Half an hour then." John stepped off the elevator, followed on the next floor by Amy and Christy.

When she reached her own room, Nikki put down her briefcase and removed the pins holding her long, upswept braid, unplaiting it as she walked to the bathroom. When it was free, she forked her fingers through it and shook her head. She stripped, shoved the wild fall of hair into a plastic cap, and entered the shower.

When she came out, she donned faded jeans and an electric blue silk blouse, picking out a matching sweater to wear over it. She brushed her hair into reluctant submission and tied it loosely at her nape.

Quickly she dusted some powder across her nose. Damned freckles. She leaned into the mirror to purge some mascara from the corner of her eye, then pulled a strand of coppery hair across her pale cheek, grimacing at her reflection. Too damned . . . bright! God, somebody was really tossing around the paint the day they decided to color me, she thought ruefully, forking her hair back into position. Michael's dark good looks again came to mind.

She willed him out of her thoughts, grabbed her ski jacket, and left. Her spirit strong, she waited for the elevator, determined she would have a good time tonight if it killed her.

"Half an hour from now, this Cinderella turns into a pumpkin and heads for home, and all the king's horses and all the king's men won't be able to put her together again," Nikki announced wearily. It was getting close to midnight and her head was splitting.

"Is that a mixed metaphor or plain old mangled English?" Christy asked, not that anyone could hear. The amplifiers made a communications vacuum of the room they were seated in.

"What's the name of this place again?" Amy yelled in John's direction.

"The Savage Beagle. Great spot, don't you think? C'mon, Amy, let's show this crowd how it's done." John grabbed her hand and they headed for the dance floor.

Nikki and Christy were alone at the table when a tall blond man approached. Nikki thought he was weaving slightly but couldn't be sure because of the crush of bodies in the room. It was hard for anyone to walk a straight line.

"Not bad," Christy whispered in Nikki's ear as he drew closer.

He looked down at Nicole. "You're Nicole Johnson, aren't you? I heard you speak today. Great presentation."

Nikki nodded her thanks.

"Bill Scott." He offered his hand and she took it. "As you've probably guessed, I'm with Prisma. California."

Nikki smiled and shook his outstretched hand.

"Would you like to dance?" he asked.

Nikki guessed he was the tiniest bit drunk, but decided to risk it. No use alienating a future Kingway distributor.

"Sure." She took his hand and rose to her feet, hoping she was right, and he was only *a little* drunk. She wouldn't relish a scene on the dance floor.

As it turned out, her fears were for nothing. He was a superb dancer with a sure, easy rhythm that made following him effortless. Nicole relaxed into his arms and was soon enjoying herself under his expert lead. She laughed with him as he moved her easily from the faster-paced rock to the slower strains of a pulsing love song.

"Where did you learn to dance like that?" she asked as he returned her to the table. The compliment inherent in the question pleased him.

"Would you believe in another life?"

Nikki looked up quizzically.

"I danced professionally for a few years. Mind you, that was long, long ago," he was quick to add.

"It shows. I can't remember when I've enjoyed dancing so much."

"Thanks. Maybe we can do it again sometime." There was an unmistakable glow in his eyes.

"Maybe." Nikki smiled up at him, but she was glad when Christy returned. Nikki introduced the two of them and was quick to tell Christy what a great dancer Bill was. Christy didn't waste a minute. In seconds, Bill was back on the dance floor.

She glanced around the crowded club. It was now a solid press of overheated bodies, a tangle of wrigglers, shakers, and jumpers, moving to music that poured from every corner of the room. As she watched, the music grew louder still, its beat stronger. It was the edge of the evening, the time when the party begins in earnest. Music, lights, and alcohol combine to dislodge inhibitions and shake loose all the normal constraints.

It was also time for her to go home, she thought. She would stay long enough to say her good nights and she was out of here, she decided. She waited for her friends to come back and continued to scan the crowd.

It wasn't shock that made her heart pound and her breath quicken. It was him. Him with a capital H. And he was staring at her.

Michael sat across the room at a table near the window. Darlene Nichols was with him and a middle-aged couple. Nikki recognized Jim Mallon, the man who handled Canadian distribution for Prisma. The woman with him was his wife.

Darlene seemed desperate for Michael's attention, even more so when she noticed his eyes fixed on Nikki. *That woman does not approve of me*, Nikki decided as she watched her, wondering for a moment what difference it would make in her relationship with Prisma. Nicole turned her attention back to Michael.

When her eyes met his, he nodded with the barest hint of a smile. The air between them tensed, like a cord snapped tight. Nikki smiled back and waved. The wave was . . . perky, she thought, and perfect for the occasion. Light and meaningless, the kind of wave one *friend* gave to another. She was proud of herself. She was the first to pull her eyes away. The room was becoming uncomfortably warm.

Michael worked to settle himself down. Dropping his gaze to the amber Scotch in his glass, he tapped his index finger on the smooth tumbler and fought to keep his eyes off her. He was successful, until he raised the drink to his lips. Again his eyes found her. He was, he admitted, fascinated. After their brief eye contact and her breezy wave, she did not look back.

He wanted to go to her, be with her, and say to hell with the damn rules. He toyed with the idea of asking her to dance but decided against it. That was impossible. He'd embarrass himself and her. He was reacting to her from this distance; for God's sake, he could easily guess the effect if those tight jeans of hers so much as brushed against him.

It wasn't easy watching her curl into another man's arms on the dance floor, sway her body to his lead. He felt like the man was touching something that belonged to him, and it irritated him that she seemed to enjoy it. She would enjoy his arms, too, he would make sure of it. But it wasn't dancing that he wanted to do with Nikki Johnson. What he wanted was to break a few rules.

"Michael. Where are you?" Darlene trilled. She moved a manicured hand across his line of vision in another attempt to gain his attention.

The loud music gave way to a quieter ballad, and this time her efforts were rewarded. Michael lowered his head and turned his ear toward her, reluctantly pulling his eyes away from Nikki.

"Sorry, Darlene. Did you say something?"

"If I did, it apparently wasn't too interesting. Not nearly as riveting as the new sales manager from Kingway." Darlene tried to joke but could not keep the sarcasm from coloring her comment. Michael was annoyed, both with himself and Darlene. It was not like him to be so transparent. He'd been staring and he knew it. He tried to cover up.

"I was thinking about her speech today. She strikes me as a smart young woman."

"She's not so young, my dear Michael, and I think she strikes you as more than smart." This time Darlene didn't try to keep the acid from her tone. Michael's face was thunderous, but his retort was cut off by the interruption of Jim Mallon, Prisma's Canadian representative.

"And so she is," Jim said appreciatively, glancing toward their subject. "Nikki Johnson is more than smart. She's one of the most talented people in the business. Frankly, I think she's wasted at Kingway. The market isn't big enough for her. I was about to tell her that, try to recruit her for our national organization, when Prisma bought the company. You've got a real crackerjack there. She'll be a real asset."

"You know her then? Quite well by the sound of it." Michael gave his full attention to the man on his right.

"Not well, but I do know her. We met a couple of times. Industry luncheons, things like that. I know her mostly through our customers. As you know, many of them in the West carry the Kingway skin care line along with Prisma Cosmetics. I assume that's one of the reasons you bought the company."

"One of them, yes," Michael agreed.

It was the natural link between the two product lines that first interested his mother in acquiring Kingway just months before she died. Megan had met Jayne Kingway in Paris at an industry seminar, and they'd had some preliminary talks. She'd asked Michael to check out the company, saying she felt Kingway had the products Prisma needed to round out its own line. By the time Michael finished his report, Megan Dorado was dead. Trusting his mother's instincts and his own, he decided to go ahead with the purchase.

Jim went on. "Nikki's a pistol. No doubt about it. My guess is she's doubled Jayne Kingway's business in two years. Damn close to it anyway. It was Nikki who set up the new distribution network. Some of your Pacific Northwest distributors already carry her products. They love her."

"Why's that?" Michael asked, anxious for more information. He wanted to know everything about her.

"Simple. She keeps her promises and she stays accountable. I guess you'd say she's an expert in plain old-fashioned service. If there is a problem, she keeps her head up. She's accessible. Those are rare qualities these days."

Darlene cut in. "You make her sound like some kind of whiz kid or boy genius."

"Never a *boy* genius, Darlene. No red-blooded male would ever take Nikki Johnson for a *boy* anything."

I'll second that, Michael thought to himself.

"A slip of the tongue," Darlene went on, her voice defensive. "Prisma does those same things, and on a much larger scale, I might add. It's a normal part of doing business. No one gives us a blue ribbon for it."

Jim Mallon smiled wickedly. "True enough, Darlene. It's just that some people, like the lady we've been discussing, do it better than others. Besides, both you and I know when it comes to distributor service, Prisma occasionally lets the ball drop. Maybe you could learn a lesson or two from that red-headed wonder over there.''

"Maybe we can." Michael delighted in hearing this resounding praise for Nikki. Darlene did not.

"Honestly, Jim. Comparing the two companies is inappropriate. Size alone makes such a comparison invalid. If the perfect Nicole Johnson had some of our problems to deal with, I doubt she'd maintain her sterling record.''

Jim Mallon got a mischievous glint in his eye. "I've been meaning to ask you, Darlene. What are those problems? What causes late-product delivery for three consecutive quarters?''

"I can tell you exactly what—" Darlene started.

"Not now, Darlene." Michael cut in smoothly. "There's plenty of time to talk business tomorrow. I think Jim just wanted to ruffle your feathers anyway. You don't want him to succeed, do you?" He tossed an easy smile toward Jim.

Jim smiled back. This Michael was okay, he thought, but if they didn't do something about Darlene Nichols, and soon, his organization would be looking for a new cosmetic line. He was glad he'd taken the chance to plant a seed or two. Although *weed* might be a better word. He would be even more candid tomorrow. He turned to his wife, who had sat silently through the exchange. "Let's dance, honey. See if there is still some rock and roll in these fifty-year-old bones.''

They'd barely left the table before Darlene started. "I can't understand you, Michael. How can you let him get away with that? Megan would have—''

Michael didn't let her finish. "Megan would have

handled it the same way. Jim is an important distributor. If he has problems, he has a right to voice them. My feeling is that it's better done in a proper environment." He turned to her, his voice firm. "I'm sorry if you disagree. Perhaps that's something we should talk about as well."

Darlene knew when to back off. "That's up to you, Michael." She forced a light smile to match her new tone. "But not right now. I think I'll visit the powder room. Will you excuse me?"

Not a moment too soon, he thought, and turned back to his drink. It was then he noticed Nikki putting her sweater on and heading for the door. *I don't dare take her in my arms for a dance*, he mused, *but surely we can stand together and breathe the same air*. Before anyone returned to the table, he followed her out the door.

EIGHT

"Warm—and loud in there, isn't it?"

Nikki jumped at the sound of his voice. "Yes. Yes, it is."

She wished he would move a step away so she could breathe. *Nikki, you fool,* she said to herself, *he's at least four feet away already.*

"Walk with me?" Michael took a step closer instead and looked down at her. The request was innocent, the look he gave her was not.

"I have friends waiting for me."

"So have I." He reached out his hand.

Without a word, Nikki took it and moved to his side. She had no idea why.

The night was cold crystal, moon bright with a sky full of drifting clouds and the fixed glitter of stars. The icy snow cracked under their feet as they turned toward the almost-deserted village center. Intending only a moment's fresh air, Nikki hadn't put on her jacket, and the bright blue sweater was more fashionable than protective. She shivered. The only warm part of her was the hand locked in Michael's, and now he released it.

"Here, put this on." He shrugged off his soft sheepskin jacket and draped it over her shoulders, ignoring her protests.

"We should go back. You'll freeze." She looked at the forest green cashmere sweater he was wearing. Warm, yes, but not warm enough, she guessed.

"The chance of me freezing when I'm in your company is very remote, Nikki." He pulled the coat around her. Lifting the large collar to cover her ears, from under the collar he held her face in his hands. "Do you *want* to go back?"

Simple question. Why did she feel the answer required so much thought? She should go back. Her friends were waiting. There was no future in a walk through cool moonlight with Michael Dorado. Nikki had never felt such a powerful attraction in her life. It was as though she were hypnotized, moving against herself and her own interests. She should go back. Get as far away from this man as possible and as quickly as possible.

"Do you want to go back, Nikki?" he asked again.

"I should. They'll be looking for me. I didn't tell anyone I was leaving."

His hands slid from under the collar to the lapels of the coat. She was trapped. Her heart hammered in her chest. Certain he could feel it, she pulled back.

"I didn't ask what you *should* do. I asked if you wanted to." He held her, snugly imprisoned in warm sheepskin.

Conflicting emotions made Nikki uncomfortable. She liked straight lines, well-marked paths, and solid plans. What she didn't like was ambiguity, unknown roads, or abrupt changes in direction. Michael Dorado was all those things, and, most important of all, he was her boss. She felt pressured and it made her angry.

"I know what you asked. You asked me for a walk."

She turned her clear blue eyes to his and added, "But it's not just a walk. It's some kind of test, isn't it?"

They'd stopped near the stone-faced wall of a restaurant. The restaurant was closed and the darkness of its covered walkway hid the expression on Michael's face, a face dangerously close to her own. She knew his eyes would be dark, intense. She felt them.

"Maybe that's exactly what it is, a test of willpower. Not so strange, when you think about it. Last night, you asked me to kiss you. Wasn't that a test?"

"Maybe it was. That was different," she sputtered, desperate for the right words. "We were going to forget about that. Be friends, remember. Besides, I didn't know you then. We were strangers." Damn it, this was getting worse all the time. She saw his smile deepen across the sensual line of his mouth. A mouth slowly moving toward hers. He tugged gently on the lapels of the big coat and pulled her closer.

"Do you always go around asking strangers to kiss you?"

"No, of course, I—"

He stilled her lips by moving his own softly across them. Nikki felt the air escape her lungs as his lips moved over hers, feather light, touching, yet not touching. The earth rolled slightly, and she swayed toward him. His arms left the lapels of the coat and wrapped around her. He lifted his mouth and looked down at her as if studying her reaction. Their breaths mingled, steaming in the cold night air.

"We shouldn't . . ." she started to whisper.

"Hush," was all he said, his lips poised over her half-open mouth. "This is *my* test." She felt his smile against her lips. "Shall we see if you pass?"

In the part of her brain still functioning, Nikki knew that Michael's test would be much more demanding than hers. This was not a surprised man in a darkened car, this was an experienced, seductive male primed for conquest.

His hot tongue grazed the moist inner swell of her lips, then moved deeper. So deep Nikki forgot to breathe. He played there, inside her mouth, probing the sensitive flesh. She tried to hold back, to deny him, but it was useless. His mouth intoxicated her, unleashed an aching, powerful need. Her head whirled, and she pressed against him. His body responded instantly, wedging her tight to the stone wall, his arousal full and hard against her. Every nerve in her body danced to it.

She freed her hands from the heavy coat and moved them hastily across his cashmere-covered chest and up and around his neck. She wanted to feel skin, his skin. Demanding more, she sought the warm flesh under his collar. She found it and a cry of pleasure escaped her lips. Her tongue met his, heat against heat.

Michael groaned and pressed himself to her. He had never felt such raw, primitive need. Control gone, reason gone, he was a hungry man. Dangerously hungry, he thought. He had to pull back. If he didn't, he would explode. He rested one hand on the wall above Nikki's head and cupped her breast with the other, his intent a gentle caress. But when the hint of one tautly aroused nipple teased his thumb through her sweater, he crushed her back to him, kissing her throat, her fluttering eyelids, her mouth again.

Slowly, he took his mouth from hers, and held her away from him, his hands once again safe on the lapels of the coat. His voice was husky and uneven.

"I want you, Nicole. I want you badly." He lifted a hand to softly stroke her hair. "It seems I'm the one who failed the test." It was as though the last sentence was for his own benefit more than hers. "The question is, where in hell do we go from here?"

"Somewhere out of the cold?" Nikki leaned heavily

against the restaurant wall, still dazed by the shock of her own responses. He turned her into a crazy woman, and she could make no sense of anything. Want. She knew all about want. She moistened her suddenly dry lips with her tongue. They felt swollen.

He smiled and ran a thumb slowly across her mouth. "I wish I could believe that was a proposition. A your-place-or-mine kind of proposition."

"Well, it's not. I think we should talk. I think we should answer your question about where we go from here."

"We could leave that until tomorrow. Couldn't I interest you in something other than conversation?" He kissed her softly; she could see a small light at the back of his eyes. A pilot light, she thought, ready to make instant flame. She swallowed.

"It was your question, and it's a good one—a serious one." Damned serious, she thought, and took a step away from him.

The game, if that's what it was, between her and Michael had to stop. The face of her old boss, Brent Marshall, bright with rage, rose before her and she trembled. She couldn't risk that again. Any more involvement with the irresistible Michael Dorado, and that's exactly what she'd risk. Pain, insults, and recriminations. She didn't need any of them. She was on shaky ground already after that drop-dead kiss. She took a deep breath. How was he going to take her rejection now? she wondered.

Nikki groaned in frustration. *All I want is to make my own way, use whatever brains and talent I have and be recognized for it. Why do I have to be cursed with another boss who would prefer that I make my way using a set of skills better used in the bedroom than the boardroom—skills I'm not even sure I possess,* she thought. *You started this, Nikki,* she hissed to herself. *You bloody did, and it's you who has to end it.* She looked up at Michael. He was still looking at her, and her stomach, among other things, tightened in response.

She found her voice. "There's an Italian place up ahead. Why don't we go in and have a cup of coffee?"

"I have a feeling I'm not going to enjoy this cup of coffee."

"They make very good coffee."

"That's not what I mean." He put a casual arm around her shoulder as they moved up the covered walkway.

"What *do* you mean?"

"I think you're going to throw my words back in my face. You're going to talk about our employer-employee relationship—and I think you're going to tell me this thing between us should stop before it goes any further. That there is no future in it, only trouble. I think I don't want to hear that."

Nikki stared at him, wind gone from her sails.

"After you." Michael pushed open the door of the restaurant.

"Would you like something to eat?" he asked when they were seated.

"No, thanks. We ate earlier."

"We?"

"John, Christy, Amy and I."

"No one else?"

"No. No one else. Why do you ask?" His questioning puzzled her.

"Obvious, isn't it? I'm working my way up to asking if there's a man in your life?"

It crossed Nikki's mind to say yes. It would be an easy way out of this mess. She could say she was engaged or at least serious about someone. She decided against it. She would accomplish her goal with truth not lies.

"There's no man in my life. Unless you count a father and three older brothers." She was glad when the waiter came to take their order. She had intended to direct this conversation, but it didn't seem to be turning out that way.

"They live in Vancouver?"

"No. My brothers are spread around the States now, and Dad lives in Denver."

"You're from Denver then?"

"That's where I grew up. I transferred here a few years ago when the computer company I was with set up its B.C. office. When that didn't work out as I planned, I took the job at Kingway." She didn't elaborate.

"Why leave Denver in the first place?"

She hesitated. "The usual reasons. The job here looked good, and I thought it was time to try my own wings. Being the baby sister in a family of men wears a bit thin after a while." It was almost the truth.

"What do they all do, besides look out for baby sister?" Nikki's family interested him. He also wanted to delay the inevitable discussion about what was between them.

"My father is an attorney. The best one in Denver," she said proudly. "Jack, my oldest brother, is president of an oil company in Dallas. Steve is the entrepreneur of the group. He owns a company that manufactures microchips in California. Corbin, the youngest, followed in my father's path. He's a lawyer with one of the biggest firms in New York."

"Impressive. Sounds like achievement is important in your family."

"I guess you could say that. I'm proud of my brothers."

"And your dad?"

"Of course."

"They must be proud of you, too."

"I guess so. Let's just say we're all proud of each other." She wished he'd get off the subject of her family.

Michael sensed his question had irritated her; he switched direction. "Do you miss Denver?"

"No. I love it here. Vancouver is a beautiful, clean city, and the way it's growing, there's lots of opportunity." Her answer was banal, but it was the best she could come up with as she tried to figure out a way of gaining control.

"Opportunity? What kind of opportunity interests you, Nikki? I know I can't count myself as one of them."

"I was referring to career," she said stiffly.

"Ah, yes. Career. Important to you. Am I right?"

"Very," she said, then added, "That's why we're having this coffee, so there will be no misunderstanding about that." *That's it, Nikki,* she told herself, *now you're on the right track.*

The waiter came with their cappuccinos, and for a moment they sat in silence.

The restaurant was getting ready to close, so there was only a scattering of people at the tables. Nikki wrapped her hands around the warm cup of Italian coffee and stared into the flames of the candle on their table. She didn't know where to begin. *Where do I begin the end of a relationship that hasn't started yet?* she mused, thinking it sounded like a bad puzzle.

"You don't mention your mother." Michael watched her and played idly with a spoon, moving it back and forth on his still-folded napkin.

"She died when I was eight."

"That must have been hard for your father. It

wouldn't be easy raising four kids. He never remarried?'' Michael drank some coffee.

''No. Maybe he never found anyone he thought could replace my mother. That would be the romantic view, anyway.'' Thoughts of her driving, demanding father pushed themselves into her consciousness. ''Or maybe he didn't have time for it. He dedicated himself to his work and his sons . . . us.'' She corrected herself. ''He was ambitious for all of us. Our success is important to him. Still is.''

Michael found Nikki's slip of the tongue enlightening, but decided to ignore it. ''What do you think? That your mother was his one great love or he had no time for another marriage?''

Nikki looked thoughtful. That question always puzzled her. More so as she grew older. Her father was a wealthy, successful, and still very attractive man. She often wondered why he never remarried. He was also an exacting perfectionist with a rock-hard set of standards. She doubted many women would live up to them.

''I don't know. My father isn't much for sharing his feelings. My guess is he felt we were his first responsibility. Like I said, he's ambitious for us.'' It was the best answer she could come up with. ''What about you? Any family?'' She determined to change the subject.

''Not close family. My father died when I was five. Odd when you think about it. You were raised in a motherless household and I in a fatherless one.'' His clear green eyes held a trace of sadness when he added, ''You probably know that my mother died a year ago.''

Nikki nodded. Megan Dorado was a legend in the cosmetic industry, and her death had been well publicized. ''You must miss her. From what I understand, she was an extraordinary woman.'' Nikki hesitated to carry on a line of questions on a subject that might cause pain. She proceeded cautiously. "She was only fifty-six, the papers said."

It was Michael's turn to nod. "And you're right. She was extraordinary. In many ways, she was a woman before her time. Today, I think you call them superwomen. Isn't that a woman who does it all, has it all?"

Nikki smiled at his use of the word.

"Superwoman." He pondered the word. "What every woman now aspires to be." He shook his head then. "God, what a crazy ambition." Then he went on.

"Mother started Prisma shortly after my father's death. She built it into an international success story—and she raised me. She was always working, always traveling. The strain must have been incredible. I could see the toll it was taking. Particularly in these last few years. I pleaded with her to slow down, but I think she'd forgotten how. By then, Prisma was everything to her. It filled her life. It *was* her life."

Nikki sensed the affection Michael had for his mother—and something else. Her next question was tentative.

"Did you resent her ambition? Did you suffer for it?"

"No. I didn't resent it. I admired it, but I damned well resent that she died for it, that she didn't know when to quit. I hate that she let her life get so unbalanced she forgot there were other things besides work. She deserved more. She should have had more." He stopped talking then and looked at her. "Were you thinking that as a child I was abandoned, left for long periods of time while my mother selfishly pursued her career?"

"It's what happens, isn't it? To have a career and family, women sometimes shortchange something—or someone. Popular opinion is that it is usually the children who suffer. Why should you be different?"

The stereotype of the career woman irritated Nikki. It wasn't necessary to give short shrift to anything in your life, she believed, as long as you worked hard and long enough.

"I didn't suffer, Nikki, nor did Prisma. That's just it. No boy ever had a better mother. I went with her everywhere. By the time I was in my teens, I think I'd been in half the countries on the globe."

"How did you cope with school?"

"A lot of the time I had a private tutor. Coogan. Actually he was some kind of distant cousin on my mother's side; he traveled with us. He had two great loves, Irish literature and soccer." The thought of his irascible tutor made him smile. "Coogan made sure I kept up."

"Where was home then?" Nikki was fascinated. What a contrast between Michael's life and her organized, disciplined upbringing.

"Originally, Madrid. I was born there. We lived in France for a while. There was a brief stay in Switzerland. Then back to Spain. I went to university in the U.S. There never was a *home* in the sense you mean it. More a series of apartments."

"And now? Where do you live now?"

"The south of Ireland, near Glengariff. At least that's home when I can get there. I keep a suite in Madrid."

"I can't imagine living in so many places. That's why I can't figure out your accent."

Michael laughed. "It's strange about that. Most people guess it's Australian. One country I've yet to set foot in. I'm surprised it's still noticeable."

"It's very slight. I like it. It's . . . lyrical."

"I'm glad you've found something to like about me, Nikki. There may be hope for us yet."

Nikki avoided his direct gaze and changed the subject. "Your mother sounds like an incredible woman. She accomplished so much. I would love to have known her. Not too many women achieve what she did."

"True. She built a great company, but she gave it all she had. Prisma is large and successful. Megan O'Shea Dorado is dead long before her time. It doesn't take a genius to understand that no one can be all things to all people. The strain is too much. The sacrifice too great."

"Maybe your mother didn't see it that way. Maybe she didn't think it was a sacrifice. She must have been proud of you, Michael. Maybe she lived exactly the kind of life she wanted." Nikki chose her words carefully. It wasn't her place to defend Megan Dorado's life.

"Maybe she did. But I can't help feeling she missed something. She should have married again, for one thing. Business is a fascinating challenge, I admit that, but there should be more to life than balance sheets and sales stats—for men and women." He looked across the table at Nikki's earnest face. Too serious, too ambitious, he thought. It unsettled him. There were so many faces like that at Prisma. Women whose commitment to their careers was at once admirable and sad. He worked with them, he respected them, but they scared the hell out of him. "But you're correct, everyone has the right to make their own decisions about what kind of life they want. No matter what the outcome."

He gave her a megawatt smile and reached across the table for her hand. Holding it in both of his, he rubbed his thumbs across her knuckles. "Let's talk about something else."

He kicked himself the moment the words were out of his mouth. He'd given her the perfect opening. It showed on her face. Damn it, he wanted this woman and no silly working relationship was going to stand between them. He wanted to kiss her, touch her, have her crazy in his arms.

He turned her hand over and moved his thumb to her pulse. Was it wishful thinking or did it quicken under his touch?

It was inconvenient that she worked for him, nothing more. They'd work it out. Besides, he would be gone in a few weeks. His chest contracted sharply at the last thought. Could he leave her so easily? He'd left women before. Surely he could do it again.

He looked at the troubled face opposite him. She was a study in innocence. Unschooled in the art of seduction and affairs of the heart. Of that, he was sure. There was no shell there, no tough skin formed over old lovers' wounds. She was all of a piece. Whole, perfect, and ready. She stirred more than his body, she stirred his soul. He was suddenly guilty about his earlier thoughts. He felt something else, too, a creeping suspicion that this could be more than a short-term relationship. At the very least, he wanted the chance to explore what was between them. Would she give him that?

Nikki's voice was flat when she finally spoke.

"This is no good, you know."

"No good for who?"

"Either one of us." She looked into his eyes, her own without guile. She tried to take her mind off the sensation of his hands. They were generating a slow, steady fire that was moving from her hand to her heart. "I don't deny I'm attracted to you. You've been on my mind constantly since last night. Even today, when I was so angry, finding out who you were, I couldn't push you out of my mind. My thoughts would make you blush, Mr. Dorado." A shy smile followed her last words.

"I'd like to hear those thoughts." Michael tried to lure her from her path, but his words had the opposite effect. Her eyes dulled and she pulled her hand from his.

"I'm serious about this. I'm sorry you're not."

"Not serious?" He took a jagged breath and leaned back in his chair. "You tell me your thoughts would make me blush, and you think I don't take that seriously. Do you have any idea what that does to me? It's no way to say goodbye, Nikki."

"I wasn't trying for effect; I was trying for honesty. I don't want to pretend with you. What would be the sense in that after I kissed you like a love-starved spinster? As for saying goodbye, that's impossible given we still have to work together."

"What do you want then?" *Will I ever get used to her directness?* he thought, trying to see Nicole Johnson as a love-starved spinster. Who had taught her to be so hard on herself? he wondered. He repeated his question.

"Tell me what you want, Nikki. What you *truly* want?"

"I want to finish this cappuccino, go back to the club, meet my friends, and more than anything, I want you and me to be what you intended us to be—friends. Friends and coworkers. If this thing between us was to follow the path of the typical office romance it would only end disastrously. Not for you. You're protected from that. The disaster part is reserved for me."

"What's between us is not a *thing,* and it's not a *typical* anything. Right now, it's an attraction, a very powerful attraction, and it's between you and me. Tell me, are you so experienced in office romance that you can confidently predict its outcome? What makes you so sure of your own hurt and so uncertain of mine?"

His words cut too near the truth. Again Nikki thought about Brent Marshall. She struggled to explain. "Be fair, Michael, you have nothing to lose with a . . . flirtation, a casual office fling. I can lose everything, sacrifice all my goals. My job is important to me. I work hard at it, and I'm good at it—and I don't want to give it up. If I become involved with you and it ends badly, I'm the one who would have to start all over somewhere else, not you. I'm not prepared to do that. It's better not to get involved at all, not to start."

For a long moment, he stared at her, a valley of quiet between them. Nikki could not read his eyes.

"It already *has* started, in case you missed something back there in the village. And what if this proves to be more than a *flirtation?* Have you thought about that?"

"You're not going to tell me that you believe in love at first sight, are you?" She almost sneered the question.

"No, I'm not. But I believe in vibrations, particularly those big enough to make the earth move. I think they're worth checking into." He reached for her hand. "Nikki, how can you ignore it?"

She pulled her hand back and didn't answer.

"I see."

What did he see? she wondered.

"Career first. No side trips and no detours." His statement was terse. "Just friends?"

"That's it." She lifted her chin.

"I'll think about it."

"What do you mean you'll think about it?"

"Just what I said. It may surprise you, but I have feelings at stake here, too. Or did you think I was faking it just to get you into my bed? I'll agree that we need time to think. Both of us have business responsibilities to consider, so I'm not going to pressure you. For now we'll take it no further. Fair enough?"

"That's not fair at all. I want you to promise to leave me alone—strictly and permanently. It's what you wanted, too. Remember? Just hours ago, it was you talking about being friends. About how impossible this was. Why sing a different tune now?"

"That was before tonight."

"Oh, for heaven's sake. One kiss doesn't change the universe," Nikki said in complete exasperation. If he wouldn't promise to leave her alone, it would be up to her. The thought terrified her.

"No. Maybe not, but it goes a hell of a long way to changing a man's mind." He looked at her, long and hard. "Relax, Nikki. Think positive. I may still come around to your way of thinking and leave you 'strictly, permanently alone.' You'll just have to convince me that's what you truly want."

Ignoring the stubborn set to his jaw and the odd green light in his eyes, she glared at him. "If that's a challenge, Mr. Dorado, I accept."

Michael smiled.

NINE

Nikki met Amy, John, and Christy for breakfast at seven-thirty the next morning, an hour before the first session.

"Niks, I never thought I'd say this, but you look as bad as I feel." John gulped down some orange juice and reached for his coffee. His normally ruddy complexion was ashen.

Nicole's smile was a guilty one. She did look terrible, and she knew why. Too much Michael Patrick Dorado. Better if her coworkers thought it was the result of too much partying. "I warned you. I have no stamina for parties. What you see this morning is indisputable evidence."

"I don't think so," Amy disagreed and gave Nikki a curious look. "You didn't have more than two glasses of wine all night."

"Obviously, that's my limit then," Nikki answered. *I never could put anything past her,* she thought. Amy gave her another suspicious glance but kept quiet.

"Can you believe the subject for the morning session?" Christy waved a piece of toast to get their attention and started to read from the meeting schedule. " 'An overview of the function and value of corporate services.' I thought these sessions were supposed to be punchy—motivational. If this is an indication of the *dynamic* Prisma organization, I'm not impressed." She threw the agenda aside, took a bite of her toast, and sighed in resignation. "Ah, well. At least I can catch up on my beauty sleep."

John spoke again. "You have your meeting with Dorado this morning at eleven, don't you, Nikki? At least that should be interesting. He strikes me as a good guy."

Nikki let out a gasp, then nodded. She had completely forgotten about the meeting. Last night it wasn't mentioned, but that didn't mean it was off. For all her talk of job and career, today's meeting was the last thing on her mind. *Shows just how right I was*, she thought. *Even with nothing happening between us, it affects things. Imagine if it were to go any further*.

"What do you think he has to say? Do you think he'll make a lot of changes?" John continued.

"Some, of course. We have to expect that. Kingway can't fit into the Prisma organization without them. As to what those changes will be, I'm in the same boat as you. We'll just have to wait and see."

"You'll let us know, won't you? What you find out today."

"Can't think why not." Nikki looked at her watch. Quarter past eight. "We better hustle our you-know-whats. I have a feeling the sleeping seats at the back of the room will fill up real fast this morning."

Christy laughed and stood up. "Do I detect a note of sarcasm in that comment, my dear Niks? You who have been so careful not to criticize the indomitable Darlene Nichols's meeting topics. At least in public. Are we to believe you are not panting to learn the functions and value of corporate services in the Prisma corporation?''

Nicole directed her best Mona Lisa smile at Christy, and said nothing.

It was Christy who was sarcastic. Nicole was rarely openly critical of anyone, particularly coworkers. If anyone did hear her complain, it was Amy, and that was seldom. If she had a complaint today, it was that Jayne Kingway wasn't here.

She was suddenly angry. Jayne *should* be here, she thought. *She should be the one meeting with Michael, not me.* Nicole was beginning to panic. How would she handle sitting in the same room with him so soon after last night? What did he expect from her? Jayne should have warned her.

Be fair, she told herself. *Jayne didn't know Michael would request a meeting. Just do the best you can and don't worry.*

Just make sure your best is good enough, that's what her father would say. She wondered why he was so much on her mind lately. *Maybe I should call him*, she thought. After all, it had been a long time. A very long time.

Nicole loved her father in a remote kind of way. He had done his best for her and her brothers. He was hard on them, sure. But it paid off, didn't it? She thought of her three successful brothers. Without warning, she felt a stab of envy followed by depression. Her father was so proud of them. His letters were testaments to their achievements, lists of their latest accomplishments. *You must be disappointed in me, Dad, a run-of-the-mill sales manager*. She felt a little sick, as she always did, when she remembered his reaction to her dismissal from VAD. ''Fired?'' He'd said the word like he'd never heard it before. ''No one in this family ever lost a position before, Nicole—for any reason. I can't believe you let Brent down that way." He assumed it was her fault, and she didn't tell him otherwise. The otherwise was too humiliating, and she wasn't quite sure he'd believe her.

"We're in luck." Christy pointed to four seats together at the back of the room. "Come on, group. It's naptime."

"Give me strength, and lead me to the exit." Christy was first to stand and head for the door.

The session was over. Nicole, absorbed in her own thoughts, had paid scant attention. She tried not to show it when she spoke. "It wasn't so bad. At least we know what to expect from the head office."

Her positive comments garnered no support from her coworkers; they were too anxious to find the way out.

"Nicole. Nicole Johnson. Could I see you for a moment please?"

Nicole turned to see Darlene bearing down hard on her left. There was no escape. She turned and smiled.

"What can I do for you, Darlene?"

"There're a couple of things I want to check with you. You and your group leave after today's sessions. Am I right?"

"Yes. Directly after lunch. I'm afraid Kingway doesn't have the resources to cover us for another day out of the office. It was difficult for Jayne to handle everything as it was. She expects us back first thing tomorrow."

"Yes, of course. I keep forgetting what a small operation you are. At Prisma we don't have that problem."

Darlene's patronizing tone rankled Nikki. She decided to ignore it, reminding herself again that she would be working with this woman.

"I'm sure you don't, Darlene." She forced a smile. "By the way, I want to tell you how much we welcomed the opportunity to be here. We've learned a great deal about Prisma, and we have you to thank. I know it's no small task organizing a meeting of this size. It's been very . . . informative.''

The unexpected praise caught the older woman off guard, and a look of genuine gratitude fleetingly crossed her face.

"Thank you, that's kind of you to say.''

"You mentioned there was something else you wanted to see me about?'' Nikki asked politely.

"Yes. I understand you have a meeting set up with Mr. Dorado today at eleven.''

"Yes?'' Nikki waited.

"Michael and I were going over his schedule this morning, and we wanted to advise you to be sure and keep the meeting short. We have a luncheon session with the eastern U.S. distributors that will take considerable preparation. Frankly, I think Michael regrets having arranged your meeting for today. Made in a rush of enthusiasm, I'm sure, after your wonderful little presentation.'' Darlene directed a full smile in Nikki's direction. "I'm sure he would reschedule it, if he thought it wouldn't offend you. After all, there's plenty of time to deal with Kingway during our stay at the Vancouver office.

"I know what you have to say will be quite interesting, but don't you agree it could wait? I don't mean to be rude, but your organization is the least of our concerns at the moment.''

Well, Nikki, thought to herself, so much for intercompany relations. Then she thought of Michael. Hell hath no fury like a boss scorned, she added for good measure. *Obviously, now that he's discovered I won't go easily to his bed, the business meeting isn't so important.* She was disappointed, maybe even hurt, but not surprised. At least now he was going to leave her alone. She was grateful for that. From tomorrow on,

Jayne could deal with him. She would stay out of his way.

She knew Michael put Darlene up to this. It was his way of letting her know what he thought of her career, a career with a *little* company. He wasn't even man enough to do his own dirty work. Seething inside, her voice was level when she answered.

"If you prefer to delay the meeting until you are both in Vancouver, that's fine, Darlene. It would be better if Mr. Dorado met with Jayne Kingway anyway. Besides, it will give the four of us a chance to leave early and miss the weekend traffic."

"Would you mind terribly, dear? I know Michael would suffer through it rather than risk hurting your feelings. But delaying it would make our time here so much more productive." Darlene hid her surprise at Nikki's easy compliance. Most of the women executives at Prisma would firewalk for a private meeting with its president.

Suffer through it! Nikki was enraged. Was she only now getting a glimpse of the real Michael? The spoiled son of a successful, hard-working woman with no real interest in the organization left to his care. Was he so bitter about his mother's death? So disrespectful of her legacy? She tried to see through her feelings, form a new, clearer picture. All that was clear was her own outrage. She'd be damned if she'd let it show.

"I don't mind at all, and I'll let Jayne know. It will give her time to prepare. Tuesday then?"

"Yes. Tuesday. Thank you again, dear. You've been most cooperative. Michael will be so pleased. I'll be certain to tell him how understanding you've been."

Nikki didn't give a damn what Darlene told Michael, but she planned to deal with at least one irritation before this conversation ended.

"Darlene, considering my favor to you, would you mind doing one for me?" Nikki's voice was sweet.

"Of course." Darlene looked wary.

"Don't call me 'dear.' "

At quarter to twelve Darlene knocked on the door of the meeting room attached to Michael's suite.

"Come in." He turned from the window, his face taut with anger. He expected the caller to be Nikki. That it was Darlene increased his annoyance.

"Sorry to interrupt, Michael. I brought the sales figures for the eastern United States. I thought you'd want to review them before lunch."

"Fine." His answer was curt. "Have you been in the meeting rooms recently?"

"Yes, I just came from there. Why?"

"Did you see any of the people from Kingway?"

"No. They left for the city before lunch."

"They what?" There was dull rage in Michael's words. "That includes Nicole Johnson, I presume."

"Yes. They were traveling together. Why?" Darlene asked innocently.

"She was supposed to be here for a meeting at eleven o'clock."

"I thought she'd told you." Darlene was arranging the reports on the table, carefully avoiding Michael's eyes as she spoke.

"Told me what?"

"When I went to confirm the meeting, she said she'd had second thoughts about the meeting today. She seemed to think corporate plans would be better discussed with Jayne Kingway. She was anxious to miss the weekend traffic, get an early start home. I hope there was no misunderstanding. I assumed she let you know."

"Well, she didn't, as you can see."

"I can't imagine why not. Of course, I've felt from the beginning that she's a bit arrogant. I can't believe she stood you up like this, Michael. How thoughtless, how—"

Michael glared and cut her off. "Enough. It's possible there was a misunderstanding. Perhaps she didn't realize the importance of the meeting." Michael felt called upon to defend Nikki, even though her actions left him baffled—and angry. Her lack of professionalism surprised him. Did she think she could treat him any way she pleased? If she did, she would learn quickly who was in control.

"Whatever the reasons, I don't think you should let her get away with this, Michael. She should be made to understand it isn't Jayne Kingway who runs things anymore. I think you should speak to her and—"

"I said, enough, Darlene." He slashed through the thickness of his dark hair with an impatient hand, determined to hold his temper. It wouldn't be fair to take it out on Darlene. It was Nikki who stood him up.

He was a fool to let her get under his skin, but she did. He should forget her. God knows, she'd made her feelings plain enough last night, though the heat in her kiss belied them. He remembered her body flush against his and those blue eyes of hers misted with passion. Why was she fighting it? Should he believe her determined words or the telling rhythm of her body?

Nikki, it seemed, was determined to prove her words. Why else would she ignore this meeting? He threw down a half-read report and would have cursed aloud if Darlene wasn't there. If her job was so damned important to her, she should be here. He hadn't thought she would do something so damaging to her precious career. Did she think he was going to seduce her over a meeting table, for God's sake! She was acting like a child. *And you, Michael, what are you acting like?* he asked himself. *A dumb, infatuated fool*, he answered honestly.

Darlene interrupted his thoughts.

". . . if you don't set the right tone from the beginning, Michael, you'll never get the upper hand."

"Darlene." He said her name with threatening softness. His eyes did the rest.

Darlene shrugged and turned back to her papers.

Michael didn't deny Darlene's intelligence, her organizational ability, or her loyalty to Prisma, but she had an edge to her that grated on him. Ever since he'd taken over the company, she tried to take over him. Early on, he'd put it down to insecurity. Now he wasn't so sure. He wondered how a new Prisma president would handle the indefatigable Darlene. How would he handle her if she hadn't been a longtime friend of his mother?

"Let's have a look at those numbers," he growled.

Darlene focused on him from under narrowed eyelids. She didn't like that he defended Nicole, but, all in all, things had gone well.

The Kingway group made the trip from Whistler to Nikki's home in North Vancouver in under two hours. Nikki was silent for most of the drive. When she told them the meeting was canceled because Michael changed his mind, preferring to meet with Jayne in Vancouver, they accepted it. She said no more. No need for them to know how carelessly she'd been brushed off.

By the time she reached her apartment complex on Capilano Road, she was exhausted. The stress of the weekend had taken a toll, both physically and emotionally. When she took her suitcase from the back of John's station wagon, she could scarcely lift it.

"You okay?" Amy asked as she watched Nikki pull her bag from the open tailgate.

"I'm okay. Just tired. More than tired—exhausted." She closed the tailgate and moved to the side of the car.

"Thanks for the lift, John. See you tomorrow." Nikki lifted her hand to wave. As she did so, she saw Amy say something to John and get out of the car. She came toward Nicole.

"Are you sure you don't want to talk? I could come in for a minute."

"Talk? Talk about what?" Nikki feigned innocence.

"Not what. Who. Specifically, one Michael Patrick Dorado, a mutual friend of ours if I read you correctly." There was empathy in Amy's eyes, as though they shared a secret. "I think I know what you're going through. Maybe talking about it would help?" Amy's face held that wistful expression Nicole had first seen when Amy saw Michael in the Whistler meeting room.

"What do you mean mutual friend, Amy?"

"I mean I understand what you're feeling right now. I felt the same way when I was in Ireland."

Was Amy saying what she thought she was saying— that she, too, was attracted to Michael? Nikki remembered Michael kissing Amy at the base of the mountain, their promise to get together and "catch up," and Amy's evasive words when she first asked her about their meeting. A shard of jealousy pierced her newly sensitized heart. Her feelings perplexed her, but she was too tired and confused to think about it. She *didn't want* to think about it, and she certainly didn't want to talk about it.

"I'm bushed, Amy. All I want is a deep, hot bath and my own bed. How about tomorrow?" She forced a grin. "We'll *do* lunch, okay?"

"I'll hold you to that. You know, Nikki, even if you don't need to talk, I do. Friends shouldn't have secrets. I should have told you mine two years ago. Tomorrow, then." She got back in the car and the threesome drove off.

Nikki's head was spinning. She didn't want to believe it. Amy and Michael! And Amy still carrying the torch.

Would there be any more revelations, she wondered? She marveled how, in less than seventy-two hours, her life was turned upside down just by meeting him. What a blessing it was that he would only be in their office for a few short weeks. Her next thought was, how would she bear it?

By the time she opened her front door, warm tears rolled unchecked down her face. She closed the door behind her and sniffed defiantly. "Cut it out, Nicole Johnson." She sniffed again, louder this time, and gained a measure of control. She dropped her bag and headed for the kitchen. "It's gonna be a long night, Miss Career Woman," she muttered aloud, "a very long night."

By six in the morning Nicole had fought getting up long enough. She'd been awake since four and slept precious little before that. *I might as well have slept with him*, she thought in frustration. *He kept me awake all night anyway*. She turned to the undisturbed pillow beside her. What would it be like, she mused, to wake up and see his dark head resting there? She remembered the feel of his thick ebony hair, the cool, firm skin of his neck. Her own flesh warmed as her thoughts moved to the seductive smile, traced the line of his mouth—

"Enough already!" she railed to herself, leaping from the bed as though it were burning and heading for the bathroom. "This may be the first time I start the day with a *cold* shower," she said aloud in frustration.

Hoping to find Jayne Kingway, she was in the office

by seven-thirty. Jayne was usually in by seven. Nicole looked forward to an early cup of coffee and talk with her about the weekend meetings. Jayne would want to know about Michael's idea for a planning session. Nikki was disappointed when she wasn't in her office.

Nicole looked around her empty office; the pictures were gone from the wall. She smiled to herself. *Jayne is more impatient to leave than I realized; she's already taking her personal stuff home. I'm going to miss her*, she thought again. *Now more than ever, since I've seen firsthand the kind of organization Prisma is.* Michael breezed unbidden into her thoughts. She shoved him aside. *Let Jayne deal with him*, she thought firmly. *As for me, I'm going to work, work, work, and if that doesn't keep my head free of him, I'll work some more.* She headed for her desk to put her plan in action.

"Morning, Nikki." John stood in her office doorway. "I'm going to get a coffee. Want one? If you've got a minute I'd like to talk to you about the Walker account. I've got an appointment with their buyer at ten."

Nikki glanced at her watch. It was eight forty-five.

"Coffee would be great, John. Thanks. Bring your own back here and we'll talk. And would you check and see if Jayne's in yet?" Nikki smiled up from her desk. "It looks like she's already started her retirement. This is the first time since I've been here she hasn't been in early."

"Done. I'll be back in a minute."

As John left her door, the phone rang.

"Nicole Johnson," she answered, grabbing at a pen rolling to the edge of her desk.

The deep, compelling voice on the other end was the last voice she expected to hear.

"This is Michael Dorado."

As if I didn't know, she thought. The cool, in-charge Nicole Johnson could not find her voice.

"Nicole. Are you there?"

"Yes. Yes, I'm here. Just a little surprised, that's all." She hoped the words weren't as squeaky as they sounded in her head.

"I expected you would be." There was an unmistakable chill in his voice, Nicole realized as her brain finally kicked in.

"Is there something I can do for you?" If he wanted chilly, he'd get chilly.

"No. There is nothing you can do for me, but there is something I was intending to do *for you*—had you the courtesy to keep your appointment with me yesterday."

"*Me* keep the appointment?" That was a squeak, she was sure of it.

"The truth, Nikki. Was it really that you wanted me to meet with Jayne Kingway, or were you afraid that I would mount a full-scale sexual offensive and irreparably damage your budding career?" The words were cruel and sarcastic. Nikki was stunned.

"Didn't Darlene tell you . . ." she started.

"Darlene told me you were anxious to 'beat the traffic home.' I believe those were your exact words."

"She told you that? And you believed her?" Nikki was both shocked and angry. She'd been torpedoed, and by a master. Darlene had done a first rate job. What she could not understand was why.

"It doesn't matter what I believe," he snapped back. "What matters is that both you and I have a job to do. My job is to ensure that the merger of Kingway into the Prisma organization goes smoothly." He paused. "Yours is to do what I say. That is, if you intend to stay with the company. I assume you don't want to sacrifice your precious career at this early stage?"

"No, of course not, but if you'll listen to me for a minute, I can—"

He cut her off. "I would prefer *you* to listen to *me*. I'll be in Vancouver tonight by seven. Arrange your schedule so that you can have dinner with me at eight. I'll meet you in the lobby of the Bayshore Hotel. We'll go over everything then."

"I'm not sure I can do that." Nikki was enraged by the dictatorial tone. "I see no reason why any meeting between us can't take place in the office during normal business hours. Aside from that, any kind of corporate planning meetings should be with Jayne Kingway." Her voice was stiff with conviction. She could hear a sigh come through the phone line. It was both frustrated and resigned.

"You may have noticed Jayne is not in today," he went on, "nor will she be in tomorrow, or the next day. Jayne is gone. Please keep that in confidence until our meeting tonight. I'll see you at eight." A solid click told Nikki the line was dead.

Nikki stared at the receiver in her hand. What was he talking about? Jayne couldn't be gone. She had a six-month contract. She reconnected the phone line and dialed Jayne's number. No answer. What was going on here?

"Here's your coffee." John placed a steaming mug in front of her. "Ready to go over the Walker account." He looked at her as he took the chair in front of her desk. "What's the matter, Nikki? You look . . . weird."

Weird was a good word, she thought. It described exactly how she felt.

"Just a little preoccupied." She covered her unease and smiled at John. She picked up the papers he'd put on her desk. "Let's get busy."

Nikki stayed busy all day. When Amy came for the

promised lunch, she begged off. She couldn't risk a cozy lunch hour with Amy without talking about Jayne's unexplained absence. It was the hot office topic of the day. Michael, damn him, hadn't told her enough to stem the rumors, and she didn't want to fuel them. Besides, he'd asked for confidentiality. She would respect that.

She tried Jayne's home number all day without success. By five o'clock, she was a believer; Jayne was gone. There was no question now about her meeting Michael tonight, and her sense of anticipation wasn't rooted solely in solving the mystery of Jayne's disappearance from Kingway. Despite his arrogance, his lack of understanding, and his heavy-handed summons, she couldn't wait to see him.

TEN

Nikki left the office promptly at five, determined to avoid after-work gossip or speculation about Jayne. She was home by five-fifteen. With two and a half hours before the meeting, and a growing anxiousness about what that meeting would reveal, she couldn't settle down. She decided to complete some unfinished work. Briefcase in hand, she went to the spare bedroom she used as a home office and tried desperately to concentrate. After an hour or so, she gave up.

She was determined to calm down and approach her dinner appointment with Michael coolly and unruffled. One long, relaxing bath later, she stood in front of her closet, a look of indecision on her face. Finally, she chose a figure-hugging ivory wool dress with a high neck and long sleeves. A bit short perhaps, but otherwise perfect. She replaited her braid and lifted it up from her neck. A dash of makeup and she was ready.

He was in the hotel lobby when she arrived. Nikki frowned; Darlene was with him. She was talking intently to Michael, and he was giving her his full attention. Whatever she said didn't seem to please him. He was rubbing the back of his neck distractedly with one hand; the other was in his pocket. Was she imagining things or did the angry look lift when his eyes caught sight of her coming toward them? He moved the hand from his neck and gave a curt wave of acknowledgment. He did not smile.

As Nikki moved closer, she gave a silent prayer. *Please, please, don't let Darlene be joining us for dinner.* She would not be able to tolerate the woman's presence, at least not in silence.

"Nicole." Michael gave her a casual nod. Without waiting for her reply, he turned back to Darlene. "Do you think we could finish this discussion tomorrow? There's damned little we can do about it tonight."

"Of course, Michael." Darlene's smile was silky when she glanced toward Nicole. "I'll see you first thing in the morning at the Kingway offices."

"After lunch, Darlene. I want to make a few phone calls, gather a bit of firsthand information."

Darlene's face tightened. "You're questioning my information? I assure you I've gone over this problem thoroughly."

"I'm sure you have." Michael's words placated her, but his sharp tone did not. "And I'm sure my phone calls will only confirm what you tell me. In the meantime, let's call it a day. As you can see, I have a dinner meeting."

"As you like." Darlene turned to Nicole. "How nice to see you again." This time the smile was pure polyester. "Enjoy your dinner then." She nodded to both of them before wafting regally across the lobby.

Before Nikki could even speak, Michael's impatient hand gripped her elbow and directed her down the hall to Trader Vic's dining room. She was itching to ask what the exchange between him and Darlene was about, but the grim set of his jaw deterred her. Whatever it was, it had ruined his humor.

At the maître d's station, Michael silently took her coat and checked it. He seemed lost in thought as he turned to face her, and he surprised her when he reached out to briefly touch a tendril of hair near her cheek. His serious eyes slid down her body, paused briefly over the curve of her breasts, then went back up to her coppery hair. He leaned toward her then, his mouth so close to her ear, she could feel his warm breath on her neck.

"You look spectacular," he said.

Nikki saw the glint of gold in the back of his eyes and felt an odd twist in the pit of her stomach. She mumbled her thanks as he took her arm and moved her ahead of him. They followed the maître d' to a quiet table at the window.

They sat without speaking until the waiter brought menus. The tenseness in Michael made Nicole wary. She wasn't sure how to deal with it. Finally, frustrated with the brooding silence that filled the space between them, she spoke.

"This is going to be an uncomfortable and unproductive meeting if we don't start talking. Would you prefer to delay it?" she asked.

"No. We need to talk. We should have talked before this. It's just that Darlene—" He stopped, but only long enough to redirect his frustration from Darlene to Nikki. "If you'd met me as planned yesterday, this get-together could have been avoided."

"You can avoid me completely if that's what you want. Say the word and I'll leave. I'm only here because you *demanded* I be here. If you've changed your mind, I'll be happy to go. You are, as you've made plain, the boss." She'd be damned if she'd explain herself. If he wanted to believe Darlene, let him.

"I wish it were that easy, but as I said on the phone, for the time being at least, we have a job to do. We need to talk about Kingway, and we need to talk about Jayne. So for the moment, let's put our animosities aside and have a temporary truce. Agreed?"

Nicole was all for that. Not only was she curious about Jayne, she found it impossible to stay angry with a man whose nearness stirred such sensual, erotic feelings. She wasn't kidding when she told him her thoughts would make him blush. Right now she was wondering what it would feel like to run her hands over his shoulders and down his chest to . . .

"Did you hear me?" He was looking at her questioningly.

She reddened. "Truce," she echoed.

Nicole could see their waiter heading toward them as Michael spoke again.

"Good. Let's order then, and I'll tell you why Jayne Kingway isn't coming back."

A half hour into the conversation, Nikki still wasn't over the shock of what Michael had told her.

"You're telling me you canceled Jayne's employment contract and she's on a boat somewhere in the Caribbean."

"Mediterranean," he corrected. "Probably cruising the Greek Islands by now. And I didn't *cancel* her contract. Not exactly."

"But why did she leave so suddenly? Why didn't she tell anyone? We're very close at Kingway. I can't understand it. I knew she wasn't going to stay long after Prisma took over, but I was counting on at least six months."

"That was the original agreement."

"What happened to change it? What's going to happen at Kingway? Will Prisma be appointing a new manager?" *God help us if it's Darlene*, Nikki said to herself. The office would turn into résumé city if that was the plan.

"Whoa. One question at a time. First, Jayne and I changed the original agreement. Much to the chagrin of the Prisma directors, I might add. It was when I was out here for the final meeting. She's quite the woman, your Jayne Kingway, reminds me of Megan in a way. I can see why they hit it off when they met in Paris. Anyway, to get to the point, we had dinner together. Right here in this room, as a matter of fact. It was the first time we'd spent any time with each other outside of business meetings. That was when she told me about her husband." Michael stopped and reached for his wineglass.

"Her husband? Ron? What about him?"

"She told me about his heart condition."

"Heart condition? Ron? Jayne never told me about that." Nikki was stunned. She'd considered herself close to Jayne. But now, when she really thought about it, she had to admit that most of their conversations were about business. Always business.

"I know. She told me she kept it to herself. She didn't think it should affect her work or anyone else's."

"How serious is it?" Nikki felt guilty and a little jealous. She'd worked two years with Jayne, and she hadn't felt comfortable enough to confide in her. One dinner with Michael and she'd told him everything. She didn't understand it.

"Serious enough for both of them to make the commitment to a different and more relaxed style of living. Serious enough for Jayne to sell Kingway and spend all her time with him."

"So you released her from her management contract?" Nikki guessed.

"That's about it. It seemed to me the six months would be better spent with her husband, getting on with that new life they'd promised each other. With the shock they've had, time takes on a whole new meaning."

"I wish she'd told me. Maybe I could have helped her."

"You did help, Nikki. More than you know. It was because of you I was able to release Jayne from her contract. She thinks very highly of you. So highly that she recommended you to take over the general management of Kingway and work with Prisma to integrate the product lines."

Nicole was speechless. Michael's face was strangely sober as he watched her reaction.

"Does that make you happy?" he asked.

"Yes . . . and no. I'm happy Jayne put so much trust in me, but I'm not sure I'm ready for the responsibility."

Michael's eyes played across her face as if trying to judge the depth of her feelings, the strength of her ambition. He saw the fire in her eyes, the pleasure manifest there. Her excitement was plain; she couldn't hide it. He should be happy for her, but it wasn't happiness he felt; it was a sense of loss, as though she was slipping away from him. He wanted to grab her by the shoulders and demand to know how much of herself she would give to her work. Would it be everything? Would anything be left for him? For them? He had a month to find out.

"Jayne thought you were ready or she wouldn't have recommended you for the job." He leaned back in his chair, one hand on his waist, the other playing idly with his teaspoon. "If it means anything, I agree."

A brilliant, clear smile crossed Nikki's face. With a stab of pain, Michael realized it was the first time he had seen her smile like that. It took a promotion to do it, he thought regretfully. The smile blazed as she spoke.

"Do you? Do you really, Michael? Your support, your belief in me would make all the difference."

"When you took control of the speaker's platform at Whistler, you earned that. I was impressed, both with what you said and how you said it. You were prepared, informative, and very professional." God, he sounded like he was doing a salary review.

Nikki was grateful for the sincere respect in his voice. "You'll help me then?" she asked directly, then seemed to stumble over her words. "And what's between us . . . You won't—"

"I won't what?" Michael did not lean forward, just deepened his gaze. He stared at her for a long moment, his eyes a cold ocean green. "Still afraid of detours, Nikki?"

"You know what I mean," she mumbled.

Michael gave her a curt appraisal and signaled for the check. After he'd done so, he turned back to her.

"Jayne said you were the ultimate professional— smart, creative, and dedicated. She also said you would never let your personal life interfere with business. You would always put your job first. She admired that about you. Did you know that? What I suspect she didn't know is that you don't have a personal life. Nor do you want one. You're wonderful fodder for the corporate mill, Nikki. Every company's dream employee. Would I do anything to ruin that?"

Michael's words stung, but she had no chance for rebuttal before the waiter was at their table with the bill. Michael signed it and stood up to pull her chair out. His eyes told her there were to be no more questions.

Nikki was troubled. Was she really so narrowly focused, so . . . one-dimensional? Why hadn't Jayne told her about Ron? Did she honestly think she wouldn't care, wouldn't be interested? The thought saddened her. Jayne meant well, that was obvious. It was her recommendation that ensured Nikki the general manager's position. A major career plum. That was what she wanted, wasn't it? As for Michael's opinion, it didn't matter. In a few weeks, he'd be gone. Better for her if he did think she was a business robot.

In seconds, they were back in the lobby. Michael again took her elbow. This time he directed her to the elevators.

She stopped and turned to him.

"Where are we going?"

"To my suite."

"Just a minute here."

"Is something wrong?" he asked.

"Well, I, ah . . . why are you taking me to your suite? she finally managed to stammer.

"To go over some information on the merger. I thought you should read the preliminary plans before we meet tomorrow morning. Is there a problem?" Michael's face was a study in innocence. Nicole felt like an idiot. Some general manager, she thought.

"No. No problem at all." She struck an airy tone. "Good."

The elevator yawned open in front of them, and Michael moved to let her precede him. When the door closed behind them, they were alone. Michael pushed the button marked seven, then lounged casually against the rail that ran the inside of the elevator.

Nikki felt the complete fool. There he was, nonchalant as you please, while she was tied up in knots. In all her twenty-seven years, she had never before gone to a man's hotel room. *You're going to discuss business plans and pick up some papers*, she told herself. *This is not some kind of illicit tryst, so act your age. Better yet, act like the G.M. of Kingway.* Placing that objective firmly in mind, Nikki scarcely jumped at all when Michael placed his hand on the small of her back to walk her out of the elevator.

Once inside his spacious, elegant suite, Michael took her coat. He motioned her to a chair near the window, but she was too nervous to sit. She stood and looked outside. The dark outline of Stanley Park and the glitter of the North Shore across the inlet were plainly visible. In the clear, cold night the lights were a bright divider between sea and snowcapped mountains. A passenger ship cruised slowly up the inlet toward the Lions Gate Bridge. To where? she wondered, Alaska? San Francisco, then on to Mexico?

She was staring at the view when she heard Michael ask, "Shall I order coffee?"

She turned in time to see him shrugging out of his suit jacket. He tossed it carelessly on the king-sized bed that dominated the room. His eyes sought hers for an answer.

"That depends. Shall we be long?" Nikki stared as Michael pulled at his tie, loosening it and then sending it to join the discarded jacket. Her fragile bravado started to crumble. It crumbled more when Michael pulled the tails of his white shirt from his pants. She coughed and turned away.

"Long?" Michael echoed with a smile, giving a final tug on his shirt. "That depends, too—on whether or not you're a quick study." His hands moved to the top button of his shirt.

"I'm a quick study. No coffee." Nikki stared fixedly out the window, but this time she could not see the view. What she saw was Michael's reflection. He was undoing the third button on his shirt, exposing a shadow of dark hair curling on his chest. She started to panic.

"The reports are in the next room. Through that

door. I think you'll be more at ease in there." He spoke the words casually, as if it didn't matter to him whether she stayed to watch him change or not.

Nikki made a hasty exit through the adjoining-room door and closed it behind her. She was *not* more at ease. Her emotions were a jumble, and she struggled to regulate her breath, which persisted in coming from her chest in short, inadequate bursts. While she fought to steady it, a ragged sigh escaped her tense throat. This wasn't a hotel room, she thought, this was a battleground. She should never have come here, but she could see no way out now.

Concentrate on the work, she told herself. *Ignore him.* She thought about that glimpse of curly chest hair and shut her eyes. Ignoring Michael would be like walking through a perfumery and *not* smelling the perfume. She steeled herself. She would do it. She had to do it, she thought wildly. If she didn't, she was a goner.

There was a round table and two chairs in the corner of the room near the window. Nikki spied a table stacked with papers. She was moving toward it when Michael came back to the room.

He was wearing faded jeans and a white cotton sweater; neither looked new. Nikki tried not to look at him and failed. This was a whole new Michael. In shedding the suit, he'd shed the tenseness that had been on his face since the scene with Darlene in the lobby.

Until now Nikki had thought of him as a cool, worldly sophisticate, too handsome and spoiled for his own good. And while his aloofness was intriguing, this jeans-clad man was more appealing and much more dangerous. She cleared her throat and tried not to notice how the denim molded to his lean, muscular thighs. It molded rather well to another part of his anatomy as well, but Nikki didn't want to think about that, wouldn't think about that. She picked up some papers and made the effort to look at them.

Michael had caught her appraising glance, and a smile curved his lips. "I hope you don't mind the change. I can only take so much time in a monkey suit."

Nikki coughed to cover her unease. "No, I don't mind at all. If anything, I'm envious. You look so comfortable." *You look incredible* was what she was thinking.

"There's nothing to stop you from getting comfortable, too. You could take off . . ." He paused, studied her, then raised a teasing eyebrow, "your shoes at least. That would be quite acceptable in an employee-employer relationship. Don't you think?"

Nikki could not keep from smiling. She had worked around flirtatious men long enough to have developed an easy skill in innocent banter. While she was uncertain as to how innocent Michael Dorado was, she chose the lighter path. She kicked off her shoes.

"Done. Now that we have both slipped into something comfortable, you, your jeans and me, my stocking feet, maybe we can get to it."

He moved across the room with the grace of a puma. He was standing beside her near the table when he asked, "What exactly shall we get to?" His voice was darkly seductive.

"Work, Mr. Dorado, work." She moved quickly to take a seat at the table.

He shrugged and feigned resignation. "If we must, we must." Michael reached across the table and sorted through a stack of paper until he found a folder.

"Start with this. It's the draft plan for product integration. It's only an outline, but it will give you an idea of what we propose. Why don't you read through it? It would be a good idea if you would pay particular attention to the section covering the coming month. I'd like to make the best use of my time while I'm here. While you do that, I've got a couple of calls to make.''

Michael left her with the folder and went into the next room. Nikki was so engrossed in the document she did not hear him reenter the room.

"Well, what do you think?''

Nikki looked up to see him lounging in the doorway. His gaze narrowed to her face.

"I think it's a first-rate plan.'' Nikki was genuinely excited. "I see you've chosen a Spanish word for the name. Belleza?'' she questioned.

"It means loveliness, beauty.'' He was moving toward the table. "Do you like it?''

"Yes. I like it. I do have a few questions. Do you want to go over them now, or do you want me to save them until tomorrow?''

Michael pulled a chair up beside hers, his leg brushing hers as he sat down. His shoulder touched hers, and she could feel its heat through the light cotton of his sweater.

"Let's do it now,'' he said. "The more you learn tonight, the better. It will make it easier for you to answer questions from your staff tomorrow.''

Michael's casual use of the words *your staff* surprised her and reminded her of her new responsibilities. For the first time that evening, Nicole wondered how Jayne's departure and her promotion would be accepted by the Kingway employees. For a moment, nervousness made her stomach tighten. She would have to work hard to win and keep their support. Everything would depend on her.

Michael noticed her pensiveness. "Is something bothering you?''

"I guess I'm a bit overwhelmed, that's all. Today I was an ordinary run-of-the-mill sales manager. Tomorrow the people I work *with* will work *for* me. It's going to take getting used to."

Michael marveled at her description of herself. Ordinary. Run of the mill. Those were not the words he would choose. Extraordinary was more apt.

"It is what you wanted, isn't it? Opportunity, challenge. The thrills and chills of unbridled commerce. The chance to use, and prove, your skills?" Michael had an odd look in his eye as he asked the question.

His derisive tone irritated Nikki. Easy for him to sneer at her career from where he sat. He was already on top, already a success. He had nothing to prove, no father waiting to see what he would do with his life. Her voice was crisp when she responded.

"I'm not ashamed to be ambitious, if that's what you mean."

"Does your ambition leave room for anything else, Nicole? Marriage, children? Perhaps a lover?" Michael's tone was clinical and his gaze open. He might as well have been asking for her color preferences.

Nikki reddened. "Of course it does. At least the marriage and children part. Having a career doesn't mean I have to give up those things. Right now I intend to concentrate on my job. There's time enough for the rest later—and I'll pass on the lover, thanks."

"Isn't a lover a prerequisite for the other two? Or do you think when you have 'time enough' as you put it, you'll get a husband in much the same way you'd pick up a puppy? Husband not to be confused with lover, I presume."

"You're twisting my words. That's not what I mean. I think when the time is right, when I'm open to it, it will happen, that's all. Right now, I'm not. So it's not going to happen," she finished firmly.

"Let me understand this. You think you can *organize* when you will fall in love?"

"If you're not looking for something, chances are you won't find it. I intend to put first things first."

Leaning back in his chair, Michael gave her a long look. "Are you so certain you'll recognize love when it comes along? What if it comes at an inconvenient time? What if it doesn't fit your, uh, schedule."

"Look. Right now . . . love is simply not on my agenda. When the time is right, I'll know, and my 'schedule,' as you call it, will allow for it. It's done all the time, you know. Career, children, marriage, husband—a woman can have it all if she's organized. It just takes hard work and good planning, that's all. Now shall we leave it at that and get back to work?" she added, trying her best to stare him down.

He ignored her request. "*Good planning*?" He smiled slightly and shook his dark head, amused at her sober determination. "What about passion? Or does that come under the heading of hard work?"

She glared at him and stiffened her spine. "That depends. With some men it's not only hard work, it's impossible."

"Like me, for instance?"

"Like you."

His smile deepened to one of promise and arrogance. "You're wrong, Nikki. It would be nothing like work. Nothing at all."

When she rolled her eyes, he grinned before turning back to the subject at hand. "So let me get this straight. You line everybody up. Kids, house, cottage in the country, big shaggy dog, and that other necessary evil—a husband—and pick them off one by one to make a neat little package when the time is *exactly* right?" He raised a questioning brow.

"I assume you've been told that you're an exasperating, argumentative man."

"Never."

"Consider yourself told." She picked up a file and gave it her full attention, intending to ignore him and this pointless conversation. While she studied the file, Michael studied her.

"You won't pull it off, you know. I'm not so sure relationships take too well to such hard and fast rules. Men definitely don't. And both can be somewhat uncompromising in their needs. A little openness, a little flexibility, might not hurt."

"Are you suggesting women turn back the clock, Michael, that women give their all for love?" Nicole sneered the last three words.

"No. I'm suggesting there's a price for having it all, that sometimes there can be losses." Michael's green eyes looked deep into her own, and his voice deepened. "I don't want you to lose, Nikki."

"I won't." And in a voice softer to match his own, she added, "I'm not your mother, Michael. That is who you're thinking about, isn't it?"

She heard the deep intake of his breath. When he spoke, his words were sure, whispered arrows that arced to her heart. "I'm thinking about you, Nicole Johnson. I've been thinking of nothing but you since we met. I want to love you, beautiful woman. Will you let me love you?"

His eyes held her as his hand reached out to gently touch the softness of her hair. Nikki's senses quickened as they always did when he touched her. In a movement that felt completely natural, she rolled her head back into the hand that was now lightly massaging her neck. She closed her eyes as he began a casual search for the pin holding her coiled braid in place. He found it and removed it. The heaviness of the braid fell to her back, and she heard a ringing in her ears as he started to undo it.

"Damn." Michael snarled the word.

Nikki shook her head, straining for the images and shapes of reality. She watched dazedly as Michael went through the door. The ringing was not in her head; it was the telephone. Slowly she regained her senses, so easily lost when this man touched her.

"Damn." Nikki, too, snarled the word. *What in heaven's name is the matter with me?* Traitorous tears welled in her eyes. She closed her lids, willing them to stop. The sheer effort of denying what she felt was becoming too much for her to bear. *He's not helping me*, she thought angrily. *He's deliberately trying to . . . to. . . .* She wasn't at all sure what he was trying to do. She was sure of one thing. She needed to get out of here, fast.

She put on her shoes and was reaching for her purse when Michael came back. His expression turned stormy, and his voice was dry when he spoke.

"Leaving or running?"

She looked unflinchingly at him. "Running. As fast as I damned well can. I think I'll do a better job if I take the report home. I don't seem to be accomplishing much here."

"I thought we were doing quite well."

"We were doing exactly what you wanted us to do. You're a . . . a—snake." She spat the words at him.

"You seemed to be enjoying what I was doing before we were interrupted."

"I was . . . I don't know what I was . . . hypnotized. Snakes have a way of doing that."

"Are you trying to tell me you were reacting to me against your own will? Come on, Nikki, be fair."

"Fair! You call it fair when you keep . . . touching me, reaching for me. You haven't been playing by the rules, and you know it. You said you wouldn't pressure me." She glared at him.

Michael stood in the doorway and didn't move. Nikki

took some satisfaction from the look of chagrin on his face. *For once*, she thought, *I got the better of him*. That happy condition lasted approximately ten seconds.

"You're right. I haven't been fair. Unless you accept the old adage, all's fair in love and war. So, how about new rules?" His voice went down an octave. "I want you, and I think you want me. So for the next month, I'm going to pursue you nonstop. If at the end of the month, you are not in my arms, I get on a plane and fly out of your life forever." A slow smile claimed his lips. "How's that for fair?"

Nikki paled. She could not believe what she was hearing. This was her worst nightmare. First he gave her a promotion, then he gave her the conditions on which she could keep it. She wasn't fool enough to believe if she spurned his advances there would be no penalty. As if reading her mind, he added, "None of this, by the way, will affect your position at Prisma. You have my word on it."

"Your word has not proven to be terribly reliable up to this point."

"Business is business. You're the best person for the job. Nothing will interfere with that. On the other hand, the fine art of seduction requires a different talent."

"And you're an expert, I presume."

"I have my moments."

"I'll bet you do. A moment here, a moment there. Depending on what city you happen to be in. The executive with a girl in every office. You should have been a sailor, Michael. Travel would have been cheaper."

Nikki watched his face. A muscle pulsed in his cheek, and he tapped one hand stiffly against his upper thigh.

"I didn't think you held such a low opinion of me, Nikki—or yourself. By the sound of it, you've had some prior experience with an office Lothario. Tell me, did he hurt you badly?''

"He didn't hurt me . . . ." *Damn*, she said to herself. She cut off her words, wishing she could cut out her tongue.

"I see." He said the words with a knowing smirk.

"You see nothing, and you know nothing, so don't go making any false assumptions."

"I see a naive young woman who makes permanent, life-affecting decisions based on single incidents. If one man hurts you, they're all bad news. You rebel against popular stereotypes when they apply to women but accept them when it comes to men. It seems to me you have your own double standard."

"I told you. He didn't hurt me. At least not in the way you think. If you must know, his clumsy groping cost me years of work and a job I was happy in."

"I assume the man was your boss?"

She nodded.

"And this was back home in Denver?"

She nodded again.

"Tell me about it."

Nikki stared at him. He should know, she thought. He should understand why she would never let anything like it happen again. And he should know what to expect if he persisted.

"It's quite simple. He made my promotion dependent on —" She gave him a cruel gaze. "How about you guess what he made it dependent on? My bet is you'd get it in one. Anyway, when I refused him, he fired me. Bosses can do that, you know. They *do* hold all the cards. It was an ugly, humiliating experience, and I never—repeat never—want it to happen again. Clear enough?"

"There are laws against sexual harassment, Nikki. You know that. Why didn't you sue him?"

"I thought about it. Even consulted a lawyer. In the end, I decided against it. It wasn't worth it."

"Why, for God's sake? The law was on your side."

"Because he was a friend of my father, and I knew his family, that's why. I taught his two daughters how to ski. I'd had Sunday dinners with them as a family back in Denver. They weren't tucked away somewhere so that I could ignore the pain it would cause. I was too close for comfort. There was no way I could disregard their feelings."

"Did you tell your father?"

"No. He wouldn't have believed that—"

"He wouldn't have believed your side of it. Is that what you were going to say?" Michael was choking on his own anger. What kind of father would not listen to his daughter? A daughter like Nikki.

Nikki nodded. "Let's just say that Brent Marshall had a way of shading the truth. They'd been friends for years. I couldn't risk my father's . . ." The words trailed away.

"Your father's what, Nikki?" Michael's voice was soft.

"Disappointment. I told you, he's ambitious for us. I didn't want to let him down. Maybe I was stupid. Maybe I should have sued, but I didn't. I let Brent Marshall get away with it because I was young and scared."

Nikki looked directly into his eyes when she said the next words. "But I'm not young and scared anymore. I would not be so tolerant if I ever faced a similar situation."

"Is that a threat?"

"It's a statement of fact."

"I'm not Brent Marshall, Nicole."

"Maybe not, but I work hard. I deserve to be recognized for what I do. I don't want that work negated by some man's leaping libido."

"Ouch!" Michael held up his hands in a gesture of surrender. "I don't know what hurt the most—being referred to as *some man* or the leaping libido part. Can't we at least call it uncontrolled passion? Even good old-fashioned lust would be more complimentary, not to mention romantic. Leaping libido I refuse to accept." His smile lightened the tension between them.

"I don't care if you accept it or not. 'A rose is a rose is a rose.' " Her voice and manner were implacable.

"Not true. A rose can mean more, much more. Coogan used to quote an Irish poet. I can't recall his name, but he was much kinder to the rose. 'Ah, Rose! You do endure/in tones so deep and bright./Blood red for passion's fire/ but white for love's pure light.' "

The words of the poem rested between them, and Nikki found herself caught in the shine of Michael's eyes. She quickly lowered her gaze. Further conversation was pointless. She'd said what needed to be said; it was time to go.

Nikki wished he would move away from the door. She wanted to get her coat; the doorway looked far too narrow with him lounging in it. *For pity's sake, it's a doorway not an armed camp, Nicole*, she silently admonished. She steadied herself and headed toward it. She was directly in front of it now. Almost there. One more step.

"Excuse me. I'd like to get my coat."

Michael did not move. "It's in the closet." He waved a hand, indicating the other side of the door.

"I know that," she said in complete exasperation. "Would you mind moving so I can get through?"

"There's plenty of room." Michael made a show of pulling himself against the door to make room for her.

"I promise you safe passage." There it was, that taunting smile.

So that's the way it's going to be, she thought. *Okay!* She drew herself up straight and started through the door, careful to turn sideways. If he laid one single hand on her she would . . . Would what? Turn to jelly like she did every time he touched her? She was not anxious to test her resolution.

The heat and strength of his body was palpable as she moved through the open door. His eyes never left her face, but he didn't touch her. Only when she retrieved her coat from the closet did he move toward her, reaching for the garment now over her arm. She protested.

"I can manage."

He took the coat easily from her hands. "I've no doubt you can. You're an independent woman. You've made that clear."

After he helped her on with her coat, he spun her around to face him. Nikki panicked. She couldn't bear it if he kissed her. His nearness disconcerted her, made it difficult to breathe. Sensing her panic, Michael held her from him.

"I'm not going to kiss you, if that's what you're afraid of." His hands burned through the sleeves of her coat, searing her arms, and he leaned closer to her. "I still want to, but I'm not going to. Not until you ask me to."

Nikki started to speak. He silenced her.

"I know what you're going to say. Something like . . . That will never happen, or when hell freezes over. I say it will happen. You can't walk away from this, as much as you think you may want to. It's far too important to leave unfinished. In the next month—"

She interrupted, her eyes full of shock. "You're not going to—" Had the man heard nothing she'd said?

"Yes, I am. I'm going to do exactly what I said I would do. Nothing you've said has changed that. A month isn't much, but it's all we've got. All *I've* got to make you judge me on my own merits and not on the tasteless, small-minded actions of a former employer." His smile was enigmatic as he suddenly pulled her hard to his lean body. His next words were for himself. "I must be a fool to think I can last a month without your lips on mine."

She pushed away from his embrace and fought against her loss of breath.

"You'll have to last a lot longer than that, Michael Dorado, if I have anything to say about it. Which I most definitely do. I didn't ask for this and I don't want it. I won't lose this time. I just won't."

"Perhaps neither of us will lose. Have you considered that possibility?" He kissed her lightly on the forehead, opened the door, and gently pushed her out. "Don't worry. I have no intention of harassing you, but I have every intention of romancing you." He looked down into her flushed face. "And if I read your heartbeat correctly, Nikki, I don't think it's going to take much before you're asking for that kiss." Smiling, he closed the door quietly behind her.

ELEVEN

Nikki couldn't imagine who would be at her door at, she looked at her watch, 6:12 A.M. But the insistency of the doorbell said they weren't going away. She gave the pillow a punch, threw her legs over the side of the bed, and shrugged into her robe. Muttering under her breath, she stumbled to the door.

"Nicole Johnson?" The young man looked at the package in his hand, then back to the sleep-rumpled redhead standing in the doorway. "General manager of Kingway Skin Care?"

What on earth? Nicole reached for the package. "That's me. To be exact, it will be me in a couple of hours."

He smiled and held out a delivery slip for her signature.

Nikki closed the door, turned the thick brown envelope over in her hand, and looked for a return address. There was none. She opened it and found a copy of the product integration plan and other reports relating to Prisma International. There was a brief handwritten note.

Nikki:

You were in such a hurry to leave last night you forgot your *homework*. I know you'll want to prepare for today's meetings, so I'm sending it along. I would have dropped them off myself, but I had the sure feeling I wouldn't be welcome. Given a little time, I hope to change that.

I'll see you at the office—about nine-thirty, I think. Would you please arrange a staff meeting for ten. I'm anxious to make the announcement about your new position as soon as possible.

Michael

P.S. I hope you slept better than I did.

She hadn't slept at all. At best, she was in a half sleep before the doorbell rang. She was miffed at herself for not remembering the reports. *He must think I'm an airhead*, she thought.

As she headed to the kitchen to start the coffee, she reread his note. At the bottom of the stationery, in gold print, it read, From the desk of: M.P. Dorado.

"Michael Patrick Dorado," she said aloud. "Half Irish, half Spanish, and one hundred percent trouble."

She was angry with him already, although she did appreciate receiving the reports. He was right about that. But he wasn't right about what he'd said last night—having her in his arms, asking him to kiss her, for heaven's sake. She'd done that and look where it got her. *No way*, she thought with determination. *All I want is to be the best G.M. I can be. When I fall in love, it won't be with my boss. It will be with someone as far away from my work as I can find. A doctor, a lawyer, a tinker, a tailor, anyone except the president of Prisma International.*

Nikki was in the office before eight. Her morning

shower had helped, but it hadn't been enough to wash away the ravages of a sleepless night. *This should be the most exciting day of my life*, she sulked, *and I'm going to be too tired to enjoy it*. Damn the man! She'd managed to review the reports he'd sent over and was grateful the plan was so good. At least they wouldn't have to fight about that. The business end of this relationship should go well. The personal part promised to be of a different stripe.

Of course, there was always the chance he would change his mind, have second thoughts about pursuing an employee who threatened to sue him if he persisted. She doubted it. He didn't seem like a man about to change course. Telling herself she could handle it, whichever way it went, she headed for the coffee room.

"Hi, Amy. I thought I was the first one here." She looked appreciatively at the fresh coffee coming through the machine. "I'm glad you beat me to it, though."

Amy handed her a cup and studied Nikki's pretty face. She could see the signs of sleeplessness under her eyes, faint gray pockets of fatigue. "You look tired. Everything okay?"

As they stood there waiting for the coffee to finish dripping, Nikki was tempted to tell her about the uncomfortable position she was in, the new job, her feelings—correction: *lack* of feeling—for their new boss. Knowing how Amy felt about Michael made that impossible. It would hurt her to know his true colors. As for her promotion, it was his job to announce it, not hers. She felt muzzled and resented it.

"I'm fine. A bit too much caffeine last night, maybe."

Amy looked at the cup in her hand. "And getting an early start on it today, I see. What about lunch today? I still want to talk to you."

"Sure. How about twelve-thirty?" She was dreading lunch with Amy, but she had promised. She didn't want to hear about Amy and Michael. Even linking their names together, as she had just done, made her vaguely uneasy.

"Twelve-thirty will be fine." Amy nodded and was pouring the coffee as Christy joined them in the tiny room.

"Mornin', all." Christy reached for a cup and smiled. Her eyes locked on Nicole. "Good Lord, woman, what happened to you? You look like something I occasionally step in when I walk my dog." The words had the right amount of shock.

The three women laughed. It was Nikki who answered, spirits revived by the warm coffee and familiar banter.

"Thank you, Christy. You really know how to make a person feel good. Tell me, are you looking forward to your reassignment to the Northwest territories?"

It was Christy's turn to laugh. "Northwest Territories, huh? I hear the place is teeming with tall, sexually deprived Mounties." She appeared to seriously ponder the possibilities. "With a properly outfitted van, the Territories could be very profitable. When do I start?"

Nikki chuckled and turned to Amy. "Remind me never to take Christy on unless I've slept a good twelve hours the night before, would you?"

The happy group was interrupted by the appearance of Darlene Nichols. The air stiffened in the room as everyone exchanged polite good mornings.

"I'm told this is where I find the coffee." She looked around the tiny cubicle as if in serious doubt.

"This is it, Darlene. Would you like some? It's fresh." Amy's voice was friendly and polite.

"Yes, please, and a cup for Mr. Dorado, if you don't mind." She continued to look around the room. At the mention of Michael's name, Nicole blanched. He was in early.

Amy handed Darlene the two cups of coffee.

"There's milk in the fridge and sugar in the cabinet," she pointed to the storage above the coffeepot, "if you want it."

Darlene was looking at the two mugs as though she'd been handed tin cups.

"They don't, uh, match," she said lamely.

Nikki heard Christy cough and knew she was covering a giggle. "Excuse me." Christy managed to suppress the laugh. "I've got calls to make. Nice seeing you again, Darlene."

Nikki turned her attention to Darlene. "I'm afraid there isn't much formality here. Will Mr. Dorado mind terribly if his mug is a Kingway original?"

"He won't mind at all." Michael's presence claimed what space was left in the tiny room. He took the mug from Darlene's hand. "If there's coffee in it, I'll drink from an old shoe." His green eyes raked across Nikki's face and up to her burnished hair. The look was approving.

There wasn't a trace of fatigue on his clean-shaven face. Nikki was convinced he'd slept like a baby. The freshness of his appearance made her feel even more like Christy's earlier description. She wished now she'd braided her hair instead of only shampooing and brushing it. She raised her eyes to meet his.

"I didn't expect you until later. I haven't had time to arrange an office for you."

"There's nothing to arrange. I'll set myself up in the boardroom that adjoins Jayne's old office, if that's okay. All we need then is a spot for Darlene. As for being early, I couldn't wait to get started. I have a lot to accomplish in the time I'm here. And while some things are more important than others, it all needs to get done.'' He smiled down at her.

"Yes, of course. I'm sure we can find an office for Darlene.'' His words didn't make her blush but the look in his eyes did. She turned to put some sugar in her coffee. She never used sugar.

"Why not the small meeting room in the sales department?'' Amy piped. "Your group can do without it for a while.''

"Good idea,'' Nicole said. "I'll go and clear it.''

"No need for that.'' It was Darlene. "I can manage with Amy's help. I'd like to do it now, Amy, if you're free. I have a briefcase to go through, and if you can provide someone, Michael has some correspondence to get out.''

"Sure. Fill up your mug, and let's get to it.'' Darlene followed Amy's friendly directions and the two of them left. Nicole could hear Amy chattering as they headed down the hall.

Now alone with Michael, she fought her impulse to escape. The room should feel emptier, the air lighter. It didn't. Determined to be casual and unruffled, Nicole reached for the coffeepot.

"Would you like more coffee?'' She lifted the pot in his direction. He was staring at her, his look warm and curious.

"No. Thanks.''

"You're sure you'll be all right in the boardroom? You could take Jayne's office. It might be a more productive environment.''

"The boardroom is fine.''

"Well, if there's nothing I can do for you, I'd·better get back to my desk.''

"I didn't say there was nothing you could do for me.'' He took a step toward her.

"Don't!" Every nerve in her body jangled out of sync.

"Don't what?"

"Just don't, that's all." Nikki moved back against the cabinet that held the coffeepot. Michael, looming in the door, blocked any hope of escape. She had no choice but to stand her ground.

Michael extended his hand to her hair. His touch was light. "I've never seen your hair loose. Only imagined it." He coiled a strand around his index finger and gently pulled it through his hand. "It's beautiful."

"Michael, please." Her heart was hammering. She gulped for breath but only succeeded in inhaling the cool, woodsy scent of his aftershave. She exhaled to regain her sanity. What was he wearing, nerve gas?

"Please?" He dropped his hand, and for a moment watched the rise and fall of her breasts. "What do you want, Nikki? You can have whatever you want."

There was a curious magic in the soft words and dark green of his eyes. It pulled like a powerful undertow, and Nikki's head reeled in resistance. With effort, she found the right words in the chaos of her mind, but she didn't recognize the throaty voice that spoke them.

"I want to go back to my desk. You asked me to arrange a meeting for ten o'clock. I think I'd better get started."

"Of course. This is only day one. There's lots of time." Again he touched her hair. "You should always wear your hair loose." Then, like magic, he was gone.

Was she deliberately teasing him, Michael wondered, loosening her brilliant hair, wearing the silk blouse with enough buttons open to tantalize him? He could barely keep his hands off her. He didn't want to keep his hands off her, damn it.

He was angry that the source of her distrust was

rooted in an experience with another man, another employer. That and her job. The all-important job!

Michael discarded his jacket and moved to the window. He stood there, legs apart, thumbs hooked into his belt, staring out at the waters of Burrard Inlet. It was raining, a bleak, drizzly rain, that poured fine and steady into the smooth harbor waters.

He knew he had to come to terms with Nikki's feelings about her career—and his own. He admired her ambition. She approached work with focus and determination, as he did. He thought about her making her presentation at the Whistler meetings, poised, prepared, and in total command of her material. She was, as Jim Mallon had said, a pistol.

She was also the best candidate yet for the presidency of Prisma. He let out a gusty, frustrated breath and gripped the windowsill. God, the irony of it! He had the power to give her the one thing she always wanted and in doing so he could lose her forever. It was a bloody cruel joke. Could he do it? Give her what she wanted most? A place at the top of her profession. A place she had earned by her own efforts. And if he did, what then? What would be left . . . for him?

His mind wandered restlessly, then settled on a vision of glowing hair and steady blue eyes. He could feel the fullness of her lips, the curves of her body pressed against him. Inhaling, he smelled the woman scent of her. His body tightened, and he cursed. Never had a woman affected him so deeply!

I'm falling in love with her, he thought suddenly.

The thought didn't make him happy. It made him miserable. He wasn't about to take second place in any woman's life, not even Nicole's—and definitely not to a job.

Of course, he didn't have to give her the position. There were no shortage of applicants. He rolled his eyes and turned away from the window. Hadn't he interviewed dozens since he'd begun the search? It didn't have to be Nikki.

"Michael, if you have a moment, could you sign this?"

Michael reached for the papers in Darlene's outstretched hand, glad of the interruption. His thoughts were leading him nowhere.

He leaned over the long mahogany table to sign the document and another couple of letters that she placed neatly in front of him. When he handed them back to her, she gave him a taut, nervous smile, but made no move to go.

"Is there something else?" he asked.

"Yes. Yes, there is. Could we talk for a moment?"

Michael had never seen her so ill at ease. "Sure. Sit down."

Before taking a seat, Darlene went back and closed both the boardroom door and the one to Jayne's empty office. Only then did she look at him. Her question, when it came, was direct and to the point.

"Michael, is there any chance you will appoint me president of Prisma International? Any chance at all?"

Michael looked at Darlene, his eyes narrowly appraising. He motioned toward a chair. "Sit down, Darlene. It's time we talked."

At eleven-thirty, a smiling Nicole closed the door of her office and leaned solidly against it. She was anxious for a moment of solitude, time to get herself together and dam the happy tears welling in her eyes. *I never thought you were such an emotional sap*, she chided herself.

The meeting with the Kingway staff had gone well, better than well. Nikki was overwhelmed at the positive response. They had applauded her! It was a solid vote of confidence. And Michael . . . ! Michael was terrific. He'd hit all the right notes. While he praised her accomplishments, he was careful to include everyone in the office. His announcement left them all feeling like it was a promotion not only for her but for every one of them as well.

She touched her cheek where he had kissed her lightly to congratulate her. She could feel it still. How special he was, she thought again, how incredibly, wonderfully, maddeningly special.

He'd be gone in a month, one short month, she reminded herself. After this morning, she was more convinced than ever that there was no future in a relationship between them. It would be a disaster for her and all the people who were depending on her. Nothing was more important than keeping her guard up.

She moved to her desk, and what she saw there surprised and delighted her. In the center of her desk was a single red rose and a card. She read it and her heart quickened. "Blood red for passion's fire."

Nikki didn't hear the first knock on her door, but the second got through to her.

"Come in." She stuffed the card under her desk pad.

"Only me, Niks. I wanted to give you my personal congratulations." Amy crossed the office to her friend and gave her a strong, affectionate hug. "I couldn't be happier. It's so exciting for you. I'll miss Jayne of course, but, well . . . I think it's great, that's all." Her smile was genuine. It was Nikki's voice that faltered.

"You don't mind then, my being . . ." she formed two quotation marks in the air, "*the boss* and working so closely with Michael?" Nikki could have cut out her tongue. What on earth made her say that? Amy appeared not to notice.

She grinned. "Of course, I was disappointed when I

found out I wasn't going to be working for Darlene. As for you and Michael, from what I can see, you'll be a great team.''

"Oh, Amy, I'm so glad you feel that way. I'm going to give it one hundred percent, I promise.'' Without warning, Nikki thought about her father. She must call him, soon and tell him about her promotion.

"You've never given any less. I don't think you'll stop now. But I didn't come in here to put more air in your already overinflated ego. I came about lunch. It seems we are going to have to delay again. The whole place, or most of it anyway, is heading across to the Bistro at the quay. It seems *you* are to be the guest of honor.''

Nikki pretended a grimace. "Do I have to?''

"You know you do. You don't want to disappoint everybody, do you?'' Amy's voice was stern.

"I'm kidding. Of course, I'll be there. What time?''

"As close to twelve as you can make it. See you then. And Niks,'' she looked back before closing the door, "I'm really, *really* happy for you. Remember, we definitely are having lunch tomorrow.''

Nikki nodded.

The door had scarcely closed before it opened again. This time it was Darlene. On invitation, she stepped inside but declined Nikki's offer of a chair. There was something different about her, Nikki thought, a sadness in her face. Nicole wondered what she was doing in her office. She waited.

"Michael would like you to move your things into Jayne's office. Tomorrow, if you can. He thinks it will be more productive if you are closer to each other.''

Nicole wondered if Darlene had any idea what Michael meant by productive. She sighed inwardly. She couldn't refuse, of course. It made perfect sense for her to take Jayne's office. She was the G.M., and like it or not, it would be necessary to work closely with Prisma's president until his departure date. She wished she could stay here, but there was no grounds to argue for it. Besides, she was going to appoint a new sales manager, and he or she would need this office.

"I'll move first thing in the morning." Nikki forced a cooperative smile to her face. "Is that all?"

Darlene went on in an emotionless tone. "I'd also like to confirm that you can be at the Kingway production facility at three o'clock today. Michael would like to duplicate today's announcement of your promotion. He wants a personal meeting rather than a memo."

Again, Nicole was impressed. Too often executives of Michael's caliber were unwilling or uninterested in making time for personal visits to production facilities—where, in her opinion, the *real* work was done. She wondered where the urbane, elegant Michael had learned such common sense. It's probably a contrived method taken from a management book, she thought uncharitably. Her gaze fell to the red rose on her desk and she swallowed. Trying to find fault with the faultless wasn't easy.

"Nicole?" Darlene was looking at her strangely.

Nikki snapped back to the task at hand. "Sorry. Yes, of course, I'll be there at three. I think it's great that Michael is making the time to go there."

"You'll find out that Michael, like his mother, always tries to do the right thing. Most times, he succeeds."

Something in her tone changed at the mention of Megan Dorado. Nikki was curious.

"Do you miss her terribly?" she asked.

Darlene looked at her in surprise. The personal question seemed to catch her off guard.

"Megan? Yes, I do. She was a wonderful employer and a valued friend—a cherished friend."

For the first time, Nikki saw Darlene's rigidly composed features soften. The effect was startling. A whole woman emerged from her carefully constructed shell of professionalism. "Tell me about her," she invited.

Darlene gave her a long look as if deciding whether or not to give her something precious. She hesitated.

Nikki stood up and waved a hand to the chair on the other side of her desk. "Please. I'd love to hear about her," she said, and was pleased when Darlene accepted the chair. "All I know about her is what I read in the papers."

Nikki knew instinctively that Darlene wanted to talk. She still had more antipathy than fondness for the woman but she could see her despondency. If it would help her to talk, she would listen. Besides, she was genuinely interested in Megan Dorado.

"How long did you work with her?" Nikki prompted.

"Seventeen years. I was close to your age when I went to work for Prisma. The company was smaller then. I started as a part-time typist. When Megan decided to go for the international market, my language skills—I majored in languages and am fluent in French, Spanish, and Italian—came in handy. What I didn't know about business she taught me, and before long I was her executive assistant." She stopped speaking, taking time to look into those years before going on.

"Those were exciting days. Megan was ambitious for Prisma. She accepted no limits, always looking to the future, adding goal to goal. She accomplished so much, and I was fortunate to be with her every step of the way. I've never met anyone I admired more, and there is no one to whom I am more indebted." Darlene's slightly formal speech could not hide the emotion in her eyes.

Nikki risked a more personal question. "She never married again. Was there a reason for that?"

Again Darlene hesitated. "She wanted to, I think. And there was no shortage of eligible men. She was a beautiful woman, as you might have noticed in her pictures. Very dark, like Michael. Somehow it never happened. I asked her about it not long before she died." She stopped.

"What did she say?" Nikki's eyes were fixed on her.

Darlene's laugh was ironic. "She said she hadn't found the time yet, but she would—soon. Soon never came, but a fatal stroke did. She was dead not more than a year after that conversation."

"You must have been devastated. You . . . and Michael."

"I'm not sure Michael is over it yet. He adored his mother. The relationship was more than mother and son. They were friends. He was always pleading with her to slow down and enjoy life. She told me he was even trying to matchmake. Megan thought it amusing that her son was trying to marry her off. 'My son is an incurable romantic, Darlene,' she said. 'Where do you suppose he gets it? From the Spanish or Irish half?'" A smile crossed Darlene's face at the memory.

"And what about you. Have you ever been married?" It amused her as well to think of Michael's attempts to find a husband for his mother. She agreed with his mother. Michael was a romantic.

"No. Like Megan, I haven't had the time, though I did come close a couple of times. There always seemed to be a reason it wouldn't work out. I guess I got in the habit of putting my career first. When I look back on the past ten or twelve years, it's a blur of work, travel, and more work. I guess that's about to change." She stood and smoothed her skirt. Her face was more open now and some of the melancholy was gone. She looked across the desk at Nikki and a shadow crossed her patrician face. She looked uncomfortable.

"I think I owe you an apology, Nicole . . . about your meeting with Michael at Whistler. It was my idea to delay the meeting, not his. I let him believe it was yours. I let him think that you didn't regard an appointment with him as important. I'm sorry, very sorry." Her chin drooped slightly and she seemed to pale.

"I know," Nikki said. "What I don't know is *why*."

Darlene raised her head in surprise at Nikki's calm acceptance of her confession, then shrugged her elegant shoulders. "I've asked myself that question, but I'm still not sure of the answer. I've never done anything like that before. Perhaps it was fear. I know early in my career, I would never have dreamed of doing such a thing. But everything I am is tied up in Prisma, in my work. The thought of losing it is terrifying. I think I was trying so hard to prove myself, to impress Michael, I wasn't thinking straight."

Nikki was confused, and it showed in her voice when she asked, "Impress Michael? I don't understand. And what on earth would you need to prove after all those years working with his mother? You must know more about the business than he does."

"I wanted to prove I was good enough to be appointed president of Prisma. You must know, Nicole, that Michael has been looking for his own replacement for months. He can't wait to get away from it."

Nikki *didn't* know. Vancouver was a long way from Europe. What was thunderous industry gossip there was but a faint echo on Canada's West Coast. She assumed Michael was president by choice and would remain so. President of Prisma International! What a job that would be. Nikki knew she wouldn't hesitate to go for it, if she thought she had the experience to carry it off. *I'm a few years from that*, she thought ruefully. *Be-*

sides, I'm happy where I am for now. Still, I think I'll sign up for a language course. Maybe someday I might . . . She heard Darlene go on.

"He must have interviewed every eligible candidate on the face of the globe. Maybe unconsciously he's trying to replace his mother. I don't know. But all this time I've been waiting, hoping in the end he would choose me. I should have known he wouldn't. Today he confirmed it. He doesn't think I have the, uh, *magic*."

Darlene had her hand on the door. "The surprising thing is I'm more relieved than disappointed. I find that I don't really want to be president. I think in some convoluted way I thought I owed it to Megan to try, but I know now I'm not the right one for the job. Anyway, I'm glad it's settled. Maybe now I can pick up the threads of my personal life—if I can find them.

"And about me knowing more about Prisma than Michael does? That was true, but only in the beginning. Michael has a natural aptitude for business. What he didn't know when he started, he made his business to find out as quickly as possible. In that way, he is his mother's son, talented and dedicated.

"I don't usually talk so much, you know. Especially on a personal level—that's something else I forgot along the way—but I guess today I needed to. I hope you accept my apology, Nicole. I would like us to be friends."

"Apology accepted." Nicole smiled, came from behind her desk, and offered her hand. "And as for our being friends, I think that's a great idea. It will make working together much easier."

Darlene took her hand. "Thank you. I'm grateful you're so understanding. I doubt that I would have been. As for our working together, we'll have to see about that. It may be time to make changes in my life, before it's too late. Besides, I think we'll both have to wait and see who Michael chooses as his successor. If it's a hard old crone like me, it might not be pleasant." Darlene smiled at her own self-deprecating remark and was gone.

Nikki stared at the closed door. So Darlene Nichols was human after all. It must have been difficult for Michael to deny her the presidency. *There he goes again*, she thought, *worming his way into my head*. She turned to the computer on her desk and flicked it on. She had a few minutes before lunch. She would dash off a couple of short memos and dash him from her mind. She looked again at the velvety red rose on her desk and shook her head.

"We finally made it, Niks. I was beginning to think we'd never get together again." Amy spoke as the two women juggled salads, coffees, and shoulder bags to take chairs in the open seating area of the farmer's fresh-food market. They sat to the side, near the window that looked out on the stubby little tugboats harbored next door.

The day was a winner, scrubbed bright and fresh from the recent rainfall, with the late-winter sun promising even better, drier days ahead. It was a promise rain-soaked West Coasters lived for and always believed—no matter how many times it proved false. On days like this when the city glittered like a newly polished sapphire, the endless rain was easily forgotten.

The market at Lonsdale Quay was Nikki and Amy's favorite place to eat. An open, friendly place, it was filled with daylight and conversation, and there was food for any taste, from sushi to English fish and chips. In a very few weeks, Nikki thought, they would be eating outside, feeding their scraps to the fat, squabbling gulls that frequented the pier.

"You know it was only last week we had lunch here,

but it seems like forever. So much has happened since then.'' Amy speared a piece of lettuce, then let it dangle on her fork as she went on. ''Think about it. Jayne gone. The Whistler meetings. Your promotion. Michael . . . I mean it's incredible, don't you think?'' She ate the lettuce.

''Incredible is a good description, and you're right, it seems like ages since we were here last. It's a challenge just trying to have lunch together these days. We started out to have it Monday, then Tuesday. Here it is Friday, for heaven's sake. I hope this isn't the usual working pace for Prisma. If it is, they'll have to trade in their general manager on a regular basis.''

''Don't kid me, Nicole Johnson. You love every minute of it.''

Nikki gave a sheepish look. ''You're right, you know. I do. It's challenging, demanding—sometimes overwhelming, but it is exciting. I'm learning so much, so fast, sometimes I wonder if I'm taking it all in— and having so much fun, I feel guilty.''

''Why should you feel guilty? You're working your buns off. It's Michael who should feel guilty. You've been in early and worked late every day this week, and it looks like more of the same for the rest of the month. You must be exhausted. Don't you think you're overdoing it?''

Nikki was stunned by the implied criticism in her friend's words. Whom was Amy knocking, her or Michael? She wasn't sure, but she mustered a defense anyway.

''Overdoing it? I don't think so. There're new budgets to finish, distributors to contact, new packaging to create and—''

Amy held up a hand. ''Enough already. I don't want to hear another word about all the things that need to be done. I've been working with Darlene all week, remember. I know the plans inside, outside, and backward. Please, I'm begging you—no shop talk.'' She gave Nikki a suitably beseeching look.

"I'm sorry. I guess working with Darlene hasn't been any picnic." Nikki was sure of that. While Darlene was more agreeable this week, she was still an exacting executive. "What do you want to talk about?" Nikki buttered a deliciously fattening bread roll and looked at her friend.

"Let's talk about the shop*keeper*. Let's talk about Michael. That was the reason for this lunch date in the first place, wasn't it?"

"I guess so," Nikki answered, thinking maybe the bread roll wasn't going to be so good after all. She'd been dreading this conversation. She didn't want to hear about Amy and Michael or what was between them. The idea of it filled her with an unreasoning envy over what her friend had shared with him. She didn't want to hear that Amy still cared.

"Why haven't we talked about him before now, Niks?" Amy prodded. "You've delayed this lunch—what . . . three, four times? Every time I bring up his name, you change the subject."

"Don't be silly. You talk like I've avoided having lunch with you, like I've *deliberately* put you off. I've been busy, that's all, and so have you."

"That's not it, and you know it. There've been plenty of times we could have got together." Amy played with her salad. "It's been hurtful, Nikki. I thought we were friends, and I thought you'd be interested in what happened when I was in Ireland. Especially now . . . that you and Michael are so . . . whatever." Amy stopped, then started again. "I just thought you would understand, that's all."

Nikki put her own fork down and gave Amy her full attention. She would make up for her insensitivity.

Amy was her friend, and if she was in love with Michael, there was nothing she could do but listen and bear it. To think Amy thought she didn't care made her unhappy. Nikki decided to be direct.

"I think I do understand. When you were in Ireland, you fell in love. Am I right so far?" Nikki tensed as she waited for the answer.

"Did I ever." Amy's silvery blue eyes misted and Nikki's heart scudded downward. "It happened during my last week there. The bunch of us took a boat to Garinish Island to see the gardens. I met him on the way back to Glengarriff and, well, you know . . . one thing led to another." She paused. "I never believed in love at first sight, but that's what it was. I spent only four days with him, but it was four days of heaven. It broke my heart to leave. If there'd been any hope, any hope at all, I wouldn't have. I would have phoned Jayne and said, Color me gone. When I saw Michael at the base of the lift at Whistler, it came back with such a rush I could hardly stand it."

"It must have been difficult," Nikki muttered as she tried to make sense of the feelings poking at her like poison arrows. "What happened, Amy? You were free, I presume he was. Why *did* you leave?"

"He wasn't free. He was engaged. What with my leaving and the pressure of his engagement, there didn't seem to be time enough for any rational thought, let alone love."

Nikki didn't know Michael had been engaged, but she wasn't surprised. It shocked her to think of him looking at other women while he was engaged. It also disappointed her. She guessed the result. His intended bride had found out and sent him packing. She couldn't quite wrap her head around the picture of any woman sending Michael Dorado packing, but that must be what happened. He'd never married.

"I'm sorry, Amy. Do you still feel terrible about it?"

"I did until I spoke to Michael yesterday." Amy's eyes were shining. "He didn't get married after all. I talked to him yesterday. He's coming over next month. Can you believe it? A second chance. You don't get those often."

Nikki was bewildered. Coming over? What was Amy talking about? Nikki's confusion showed on her face when she asked, "Who's coming over?"

"Sean." It was Amy's turn to be confused.

"Who's Sean?"

Amy rolled her eyes. "You're working too hard, Nikki. I've been telling you all about him. Haven't you been listening?"

"Of course, I've been listening. I thought you were talking about—" Nikki was too embarrassed to continue.

"About who, for heaven's sake?" Amy was genuinely puzzled.

Nikki had no escape. "I thought you were talking about Michael Dorado."

"What? You're kidding. Why would you think that?" Amy laughed. "Michael is Sean's cousin. That's how I met Michael. Sean introduced us one night at the local pub. We shared 'a couple of pints' and had dinner with him."

"Didn't he think it strange Sean was with you when he was engaged to another woman?"

Amy gave a slight shrug. "If he did, he didn't let on. Or Sean and I didn't notice. Sean did tell me Michael wasn't very fond of his fiancée. Maybe that had something to do with it. Anyway, the real story is that Michael called Sean after we talked this week and arranged for him to come over. I can't wait for you to meet him, Niks. If you think Michael is a dish, wait until you see Sean.''

"I never said Michael was a dish," Nikki was quick to retort. "I don't think of him that way. I think of him as my boss."

"Yeah, right," Amy drawled. "You mean you haven't noticed the fully loaded six-foot frame that would be every woman's fondest wish?"

Nikki remained silent and tried to look unconcerned.

Amy continued. "And you haven't noticed the pair of sexy green eyes that seem only able to focus on you no matter how many women are in the room? If that's true, you need serious help. You are one sick woman."

"I don't know what you're trying to say, Amy." Nikki tried for a huffy tone.

"What I'm saying is you should take the time to smell the flowers. Particularly that red rose that has come every day this week." Amy smiled knowingly and reached for the bill. "C'mon, let's go. My desk looks like Mount Everest, and I intend to clear it before this day is out.''

_____ TWELVE _____

The next week was as busy as the first. A blur of meetings topped with a zillion phone calls. The hardest part was the contract discussions with one of Prisma's biggest distributors. They'd been difficult, she thought, but Michael had handled it beautifully. Her shortest workday in the past two weeks was ten hours. Even at this pace, Nikki despaired of getting everything done before Michael had to leave. Two weeks, she thought. Two short weeks. She didn't like to think about that. She closed her office door and sagged against it. Amy was right, she was pushing too hard.

I never thought I'd say it, she thought, *but thank God it's Friday. Tonight, I'll be out of here by seven and in bed by nine, where I intend to stay until Sunday afternoon.*

She was plain bushed, more than she wanted to admit. She'd been honest with Amy when she told her she was loving every minute of it, but it wasn't without strain. A strain mostly caused by one Michael Dorado.

Nikki was more drawn to him every day, and she couldn't understand why. He'd been a perfectly proper employer, not to mention an exciting and challenging boss. He had made no move, and there sure wasn't any sign of the promised romance. Nikki frowned. Still, it was as though he was reining her in, encircling her with an invisible golden cord. He was doing *something*. She didn't know what.

What *was* he doing?

Nikki half sat on the front of her desk, engrossed in the puzzle.

There was the red rose, of course. It came every day, but since the first day never with a card. She'd told him to stop the roses. He'd ignored her.

There was his smile. He always smiled at her in that strangely warm, sensual way. But that could be her imagination. He smiled at everyone, easily and often, she noticed. You can't tell a man to stop smiling at you. That would be stupid.

What about his touching her? Nikki thought about that. He did tend to touch her once in a while, but it never seemed out of place, and it was never when they were alone. It wasn't unusual for him to place a hand on her shoulder when he leaned over her desk to study something or to touch the small of her back as he stepped back to let her through a door or into an elevator. Common courtesy. That couldn't be it. He *had* hugged her once, when they'd finalized that troublesome distributor agreement. But he'd been careful not to prolong it. Nikki remembered with absolute clarity just how damn short that hug was.

What exactly was he guilty of? Why did she feel she was being romanced when she could see no evidence of it? Her frown deepened.

He *had* touched her hair again. She was sure of it. Yesterday, when it was down. He'd come in carrying two cups of coffee and moved behind her desk to look at the sales projections. He *had* stroked it ever so lightly. Or was she dreaming? She'd been dreaming a lot this week.

There was one other thing, and when she thought of it, Nikki felt the golden cord tighten across her chest. The scent of him in the morning! That clean, potently male scent accented with an aftershave chaser. If she closed her eyes right now and breathed deep, she could smell it.

I'm falling in love with him, she thought suddenly. *I know I am. Minute by minute, hour by hour, day by day, I'm falling for the guy and he hasn't done anything but be himself.* The thought frightened and excited her.

Shake loose, woman, shake loose. Those kinds of thoughts are exactly what he wants you to think. Next thing you know, it will be you wanting the office romance. Besides, there's a big difference between falling and fallen. A very big difference.

Nikki determinedly grabbed hold of her senses. Michael was winning. She wanted to fight back, but she couldn't for the life of her find the enemy.

She moved from the uncomfortable edge of her desk to the comfort of the swivel chair behind it. She spun it to face the wall and closed her eyes. Flexing her shoulders, she worked to ease her tight back muscles and push Michael from her mind. *A long, hot bath, that's what I need. With the works—bubbles, oil, foaming water.* She thought longingly of her Jacuzzi tub at her apartment, her eyes still closed, still working her shoulder muscles. She didn't hear the footsteps behind her until it was too late.

Two strong flexible hands found their way under the mane of her loose hair and massaged her shoulders.

"Sleeping on the job?" Michael's voice teased.

Nikki tried to wrench herself away, but his hands held her.

"Don't—" she started to say.

"Relax, Nikki, I know how tired you must be. It's been a long week. And can't you think of anything else to say besides 'don't'?" His hands gentled her as they kept up their assault on her tired, tense muscles, muscles that had tensed even more at the first touch of his hands.

"You shouldn't be here." The objection was a lame one as she allowed his fingers to probe and prod the stress knots near the nape of her neck. It felt so good, she could scarcely stand it. Still, she had programmed herself to protest. "You said you wouldn't—"

"Kiss you. I said I wouldn't kiss you, and I won't. I think I've been a model lecher for two weeks. As for this . . ." He rested his broad palms on her shoulders and used his thumbs to ease the ache of fatigue lodged between her shoulder blades. "This is not kissing, this is a company benefit. Nothing personal, you understand. It's a service I offer to all my general managers."

"Sure, you do." Nikki's words were a sarcastic sneer. *Why don't I get up and throw him out of here?* she asked herself. *He is giving me good reason, isn't he?* Instead, she found herself leaning back into his hands, reveling in the heat and gentleness of his touch.

As he worked to loosen the tight cords of her neck with his thumbs, the palms of Michael's hands settled on her shoulders near the base of her neck. His long fingers rested on her collarbone. Nicole could feel the weight of him when he leaned down to bring his mouth to her ear. His warm breath against her neck made her shudder, and she moved her head to give his mouth easier access to the line of her throat.

"You believe me, Nikki? I'm surprised. I thought you had me pegged as another office Romeo. Can I assume we're making progress?" His lips caressed her neck and every fiber of her femininity responded. A long sigh escaped her lips. His hands were so good, his lips so soft, everything was so right. She could feel his hands moving down her shoulders, only the silk of her blouse between them and her sensitized skin. His breath on her neck seared her flesh. If she was to turn ever so slightly, she could take in the smell of him, taste him . . .

Somewhere in the morass of her feelings, Nikki found her bearings. Her eyes glazed and confused, she turned her chair so she could face him and then pushed away. This was madness, pure and simple. He was driving her crazy. And when she looked up into his darkened, smiling eyes, she knew he knew it. *Damn him*, was her next thought. *This is ridiculous. He's not irresistible. No more so than any other man.*

"You're not going to give up, are you?" Nikki struggled for control.

"No." He moved back and leaned, half sitting, half standing against her desk. "I have too much to gain if I win." Michael watched intently as emotions fast-forwarded themselves across the delicate features of her face. He was glad she pulled away. Making love to Nicole Johnson in her office wasn't exactly what he had in mind. *But you would have*, he said to himself. One more minute kissing that creamy throat and you damn well would have. He swallowed—hard.

Nikki's mind was in overdrive. There was no way she could take another two weeks of this. She was fighting with one hand tied behind her back. She thought of all the times she had easily warded off other men's unwelcome advances. But that was when she was on equal ground with nothing to lose. Michael was different. *Boy, is he different*, her little voice echoed. She'd never heard her little voice leer before. She shook it away.

He was her boss. She couldn't just brush him off

like a piece of lint. It wouldn't be right. *You're not too sure you want to, Nicole. That's the real problem.* It was her rotten little voice again. *Be still,* she told it. *I've got to think.* If only she could make it his idea. But how?

It seemed to Nikki that so far in this relationship, Michael won every meet, while she went nowhere at warp speed. If she didn't do something to even the odds, it would become intolerable. *I will not be hunted like a nervous rabbit,* she thought. Her creative mind sought an alternative. If not the hunted, what? A sly smile crossed her face. What had Megan Dorado said about her son; he was an incurable romantic? She got up from her chair and looked at her handsome adversary.

"Why don't you buy me dinner tonight, Michael, and we'll talk about it? About us." The surprise registered on his face delighted her. *Gotcha,* she said to herself with glee. Still, there was caution in his voice when he answered.

"Dinner is a great idea." He watched her.

"Good. But I want to go home first. Can we meet later? There's a terrific Italian place on Marine Drive. La Cucina. Around the 1900 block, I think. Say about eight-fifteen?"

Michael looked wary, but he glanced at his watch and nodded his assent. He, too, would have time to go back to the hotel for a quick shower and change of clothes.

"I hope it's casual."

"It is. Wear something you're comfortable in." She reached for her bag and walked around him to the door of her office, then looked back. "Something easy to get out of."

Nikki had only a second to register Michael's expression before she closed her door. Shock was not a strong enough word.

Nikki was home in fifteen minutes. Within fifteen minutes of that, she was showered and anxiously rummaging through her closet.

This wasn't going to be easy, but it was important she look the part. The trouble was she didn't have any office vamp clothes. She hadn't realized until now how conservative her wardrobe was. In desperation, she chose a short black skirt, black stockings, and black high heels—very high heels. She looked at them dubiously. Her back would probably be out for days. She topped it with a deep turquoise silk blouse, leaving only enough buttons closed to avoid arrest. For accessories, she dug out her old jewelry box and found a set of noisy bangles—too many—and large drop earrings.

Hair, she thought. *What should I do with my hair?* She tried pushing it to one side and thought it looked too chaste. She fiddled some more, then swept its copper abundance up from her nape into an artfully mismanaged fountain of wisps, curls, and tendrils that fell in profusion around her face. *Probably into my pasta, too*, she thought ruefully. She used twice her normal makeup, all courtesy of Prisma, stood back, and studied the effect. She choked back a laugh. *I've done it*, she said. *I'm the perfect office sex machine . . . I hope no one sees me* was her next thought.

Nikki wasn't sure where this charade would lead, but she felt good she had at least taken a bit of control. Before leaving her apartment, she spent a few minutes fixing her objective for the evening firmly in her mind. She was determined to make Michael see the same futility in an office relationship she saw herself, the plain, untouched truth about what it was like when a boss and an employee became involved. If he was a romantic, as she and his mother believed, he would not like the new, recently updated Nicole Johnson. If she was lucky, he would run for his life.

Nikki took a last look in the mirror and added another shot of mascara to her long lashes. In her wildest imaginings, she couldn't see the suave, urbane Michael Dorado escorting this woman in public. She rubbed her lips together to set the brilliant red of her lipstick. *It's a good thing he's young and strong,* she thought. *If he wasn't and he looked at me, he might have a heart attack!*

With that, she donned her coat and left.

Nikki was ten minutes late getting to the restaurant.

"I'm meeting a gentleman. Dark hair. Tall." The maître d' was helping her off with her coat.

"Mr. Dorado?"

She nodded and slowly followed his lead to a table at the back of the restaurant, staying far enough behind for Michael to get the full effect. Shoulders high, she concentrated on producing an undulating, rhythmic walk. It wasn't easy in the four-inch stiletto heels. Too late, she remembered why they were in the back of her closet; they were killing her! She sent up a silent prayer: *Please let me get to the table without falling on my face.*

Michael watched Nicole's entrance with astonishment. What had she done to herself? First, the unexpected invitation to dinner. Now this? Every eye in the room was on her. One thing was for sure; if she had decided to break her rule, she was planning to do it with a vengeance. He wished that was the case, but guessed otherwise. With Nikki, it wouldn't be that simple.

He continued his scrutiny as she approached the table and felt a tensing in the pit of his stomach. She was pure seduction. Her appearance, which he knew was carefully calculated, was hot and sultry. Heavy-handed? Maybe, but sexy as hell. His eyes drifted over her: the glistening mass of hair, the open neckline of her blouse, the erotic curve and sway of her hips, and fixed finally on the dark silk of her legs. He imagined what she would wear under such an outfit. At the thought, it was no longer only his stomach feeling tense. He stood up as she reached the table.

"Hello, Michael. Sorry I'm late." Nikki gave him a dazzling smile. Leaning forward, she let her blouse gape open as she kissed him lightly on the cheek. She would get and keep control of this evening. That meant capturing Michael's interest and holding it. She glanced up at him from carefully lowered lashes. For a few seconds she faltered. She could not read his eyes. In the dim light, they were no longer emerald but black opals, the green hidden in dark ebony depths, depths that held in check a man's restrained and ardent passion.

"No problem. I just got here myself. I ordered wine, but I can get you something else if you prefer." They took their seats.

"Wine will be perfect," she gushed.

The waiter arrived promptly to fill their glasses. As he worked with the cork, he commented on Michael's wine selection. Temporarily taking his eyes off Nikki, Michael turned to the waiter. She breathed a sigh of relief and leaned back in her chair, but she couldn't take her eyes off the man across from her.

He was dressed simply—black slacks and a soft black sweater, the starkness broken at the neck by the collar of a deep red striped shirt. He looked dramatic and sensual. As usual, he wore no jewelry except for a watch. His straight black hair was thick and shining. Sitting back comfortably in his chair, he exuded the easy grace Nikki had come to admire.

For a moment, his attention left the chattering waiter, and he looked at her, possessing her with an impatient, intimate smile. His smile made her tremble. She reached for her wine, but her eyes remained locked on the relaxed, darkly appealing man across from her. A wave of physical attraction overwhelmed her. For a moment, she was afraid. *I'm out of my league here, way out of my league.* She wanted to run, but her die was cast. She would see this night through if it killed her. As well it might, she thought miserably.

"I thought he'd never go," Nikki said, and forced a bright smile to her nervous mouth.

"Sorry. I didn't mean to ignore you." Michael drank some wine and openly studied her before he spoke again, glancing up to the wild tumble of red hair as he did so. "You look . . . different tonight."

"Do I?" she replied innocently. "In what way?"

"Kind of an interesting cross between the Happy Hooker and Little Orphan Annie. Appealing, though. Especially the Happy Hooker part. Tell me, is there a message in all this, the offer of dinner and the, uh," he burned a look toward the opening of her blouse, "other invitation. It is an invitation, isn't it? If it's not, you should be warned that you're playing with fire."

Nikki fixed what she hoped was a mysterious smile on her face and slowly raked the back of his hand with a painted nail.

"Michael, how cruel you are. Happy Hooker indeed! How can you say such a thing? I'm trying to please you. I want to be exactly what you want me to be. Did I do something wrong?"

Michael was warming to the game. "Let me get this straight. You want to please me. Is that it? That's what this is all about?"

"Of course. What else could it be?" Nikki took a breath for courage and lifted her foot out of her shoe.

She began rubbing it against Michael's calf. She couldn't believe she was doing it, but she was. What was irritating was, it didn't seem to be bothering him one bit.

"If you want to please me, love, the foot should go higher, much higher." A wicked smile crossed the chiseled planes of his face.

Nikki was saved from responding by taking another drink of wine and the return of the waiter to take their order. He'd called her love! She hadn't expected that. Determined as she was to control this evening, she could feel that control slipping away. *I should have remembered the effect he has on me*, she thought, *and that he's as stubborn as I am*. He wasn't about to make this easy.

"I thought we should talk about your travel schedule."

"My travel schedule?" he repeated.

"Yes. How often do you plan on being in Vancouver? I know it's not romantic, darling, but I do want to have an idea when you'll be flying in. You know, so I can arrange my life accordingly."

"Nikki, what are you talking about?" He liked her calling him darling, he decided. So she was being facetious. Sincerity would come later, he would see to that. He liked her touching his hand, too, and moving her foot against his leg, he liked everything about this sassy woman. He couldn't wait to see what she would come up with next. He settled back in his seat with the pure aim of enjoying himself.

She ignored his question and carried on. "You're definitely not married, are you?" She seemed to think about this for a minute or two. "Because if you are, we'll have to be much more careful, of course. Not to worry, we can handle it, I'm sure." She gave him a wonderfully seductive smile. "We all know that love, true love, conquers all. Isn't that right?"

"Right." He smiled back, not giving an inch.

"We'll have to be careful in the office, of course. I'll get a lock for my office door. In case we . . ." She let her voice trail off to a raspy whisper and looked at him through lowered lashes. "And I think I should get a private line, don't you? I know it's an extra cost for the company, but it will make it easier for us to make our arrangements."

"Oh, yes. Definitely a private line and *most definitely* a lock for your office door—and maybe a new couch?"

Nikki refused to look at him then, keeping her head down as if to think of anything else that should go on the list. "Let's see, you'll need a key to my apartment . . . and I'll need a substantial travel budget." Again she gave him a lingering smile. "There may be times when we *have* to get away. I'll try not to be too demanding, darling, but I will want as much of you as I can get." She raised her eyes to his face as she spoke the last sentence.

Don't I wish, he said to himself as he nodded. "Of course."

"Oh, and Michael, I'll try not to let my job get in the way of our relationship. Of course, I'll understand if yours does. I mean that's different, isn't it?"

So she intended to give him an object lesson. And a damned effective one. This feisty lady never did anything in half measures. In living color she was depicting her vision of what a relationship between them would be like. It was not a pretty sight, he thought grudgingly. No wonder she was giving him a wide berth. *If you only knew, Nikki, how wrong you are!*

He locked his green eyes on her and marveled again at the delicacy of her features, the high proud chin, intelligent blue eyes, and her brilliant hair. And her mouth . . . Michael's breath set in his throat. Along with the surge of desire came a wave of exasperation. *I'm such a fool for this woman*, he thought, *I'm liable to take whatever she offers*. His eyes moved to the shadowy valley between her breasts, and he shifted uncomfortably in his chair. There was powerful chemistry at work here, chemistry well beyond the minimum required for an office romp. He intended to make her see that.

She was smart, determined, and bold, more of a match for him than any woman he'd ever known, but she misjudged one thing—the depth of what he felt for her. She was dead wrong about him, and he intended to stick to his plan and prove it. Right now there was only one course of action open to him. She'd had her fun. Now it was his turn.

Their dinner orders came, and he kept his eyes on Nikki while the waiter placed the plates and sprinkled Parmesan cheese over their two orders of tortellini. To Michael, the room had become smaller, the air heavier. Looking at her shortened his breath. If it was a game she wanted, a game she would get. Hell, he might even enjoy it.

"I never thought you would be so tolerant, Nikki. You're proving to be more understanding than I thought. You're right about the private line and the increased travel budget. A trip now and then does help to keep the passion alive. Although with you and me, I don't expect that to become a problem."

He turned his hand under her still-softly-raking nails and took her hand firmly in his. Gently, he caressed her palm before letting his thumb rest on the pulse of her wrist. There was no mistaking its pace, and he smiled knowingly into her eyes before he went on. "About the key to your apartment, could you have it cut tomorrow? We don't have much time, and I'm not a patient man. I want you, love. As much and as often as I can have you—and as soon as possible.''

Nikki was caught by the deep, masculine timbre of his voice. It was her turn to be wary. She managed a weak smile and tried to check the flash fire that burned up her arm. The man's touch was like lit kerosene, and the look in his eyes was dangerous. When she tried to pull back her hand, he tightened his grip.

"You want me, too, don't you?" he asked, moving his other hand slowly up the silk of her forearm.

She was losing it! She could feel the events of the evening slipping from her charge, and she was beginning to feel dizzy. The heat of his eyes and the burning trail of his touch disoriented her. If only he'd stop looking at her like that. She had to make him stop looking at her.

"Michael, please, I would like—" Nikki wondered what exactly she would like. She couldn't think. Her head was filled with smoke and wind, and she was warm, too warm.

"What, Nikki? What do you want?"

"Another glass of wine, I'd like another glass of wine." She managed to free her hand. It was Nikki who reached for the wine bottle.

"Do you usually drink this much wine with dinner? Or am I making you nervous?"

"Nervous? Me? Of course not." It wasn't nervousness Nikki was feeling. It was raging hormones. Maybe an extra glass of wine would help her get through this dinner. She picked halfheartedly at the creamy pasta. The tortellini was, as usual, up to standard. Her appetite wasn't.

Nikki hadn't known exactly what to expect from Michael when she planned this demonstration. What she hoped was that he would be embarrassed, maybe even angry. She hadn't expected he would regard her as his evening's entertainment. He was enjoying every minute of this. The niggle of a question formed in her mind. There was no way he believed what she said, was there? Nikki felt threads of panic lacing themselves through her rib cage. *He couldn't possibly have believed me!* No matter, she couldn't allow him to get the better of her. She sipped her wine, hoping it wouldn't have its usual effect and make her sleepy.

It was Michael who spoke next.

"I'm glad you're not nervous because there is something else we should discuss. Now that I see you're so open about everything." He paused to give her a joltingly seductive smile, then raised a questioning eyebrow. "But it is delicate."

"Delicate?" Nikki eyed him suspiciously and drank her wine, although her head was dangerously foggy already. "What do you mean, delicate?" She poured the last of the wine into her glass.

Michael appeared to reconsider but kept an eye on her as he spoke. "I think we'd better forget it. It takes considerable sophistication to openly discuss certain aspects of a new relationship, and I wouldn't want to embarrass you. I'm a bit of a detail man when it comes to certain things. You may have noticed that. I like to know what to expect. Still, if you mean what you say about wanting to please me. . . ."

He was casually turning their empty wine bottle upside down and placing it back in the ice bucket to the side of their table. He didn't intend to order more.

"Embarrass me? Don't be foolish. I'm not a complete innocent, you know. Now what is it you want to talk about?" The wine gave Nikki a solid shot of courage. She could handle this, no problem.

"You're sure?" Michael speared a tortellini.

"I'm sure," she said, trying in vain to get back into character. Maybe she was getting just a bit sleepy. "I like to think you and I will be able to talk about anything. Now what is it you want to discuss.''

"Sexual practices. What I like, what you like. Where and how often. That kind of thing. Don't you think a man and a woman should—''

Nikki choked on her wine. As she coughed, sputtered, and gasped for breath, Michael left his chair and came to her aid; so, too, did the waiter and maître 'd. Now she wasn't only entertaining Michael; her audience was the whole restaurant.

The three men took attentive positions around her back as she fought to regain her lost composure. After a couple of deep, satisfying breaths she glanced up at Michael. There was no mistaking the humor in his eyes. He was definitely laughing at her. Sexual practices, indeed!

"Please sit down, Michael.'' She glared at him and then looked as pleasantly as her foggy head would allow at the hovering restaurant staff. "I'm fine now. Thank you.''

When they left, she turned to her dinner companion.

"You enjoyed that, didn't you?'' she hissed.

"I've enjoyed the whole evening so far, but judging by the tone of your voice, it sounds like the fun's over.''

"You're right about that.'' Nikki blew at a tendril of her long hair that had fallen across her face. With an impatient hand, she brushed it aside and reached for her glass.

"Don't you think you've had enough?''

Nikki gave him a stubborn look and took another drink. There was no way he was going to tell her what to do. Who did he think he was, anyway? Nikki looked at the food on her plate. When did that come? She didn't remember ordering any food. A tear coursed down her cheek; she brushed it away with the back of her hand. She felt wretched and tired. Damn the wine.

This evening had not gone the way she wanted it at all. She'd made a complete jackass of herself. She clenched her teeth and tried to raise her eyes to the man sitting across from her. She had to look strong, like she could take it. Wasn't that right? When she finally got her eyes to focus, she could see Michael was smiling. She wanted to read the smile. Was it kind, mocking, self-satisfied? She couldn't tell. Her eyes felt heavy; she dropped them and stared at the tablecloth. Maybe another sip of wine would clear her head.

When Michael saw Nikki reach for the wine, he decided the game was over. He could see she wasn't used to drinking. He stayed her hand and stood up.

"Come on. Let's get out of here."

Nikki felt an arm go around her. A strong, friendly arm. It felt nice. Kind of cozy and reliable. She liked it, but she wasn't ready to go. She wanted to think something through. She couldn't remember what it was, but she knew it was important. She also wanted to sleep.

"Do you think you can stand up?" The nice voice sounded like it cared, and now both arms were around her. It was Michael's voice, Michael's arms. So good. What was he saying? Something about standing up? She rose uneasily to her feet. If Michael asked her to stand up she would. She wanted to please him. Isn't that what she said? Isn't that what she set out to do?

THIRTEEN

Michael opened the restaurant door and helped Nikki outside. The cold night air brought some order to her addled senses, but she was still numb and surprisingly weak. All she could think of was getting home and going to bed. She fumbled for her car keys.

"What do you think you're doing?" he demanded.

"I'm looking for my keys. What do you think I'm doing?"

"I think you're crazy if you believe for a second I'm going to let you drive anywhere."

"And how do you think you're going to stop me?" Nikki stuck her chin out and kept digging for the keys.

"By force if necessary." Michael's face was grim. "You know damn well you're in no condition to drive. Come with me."

Ignoring her struggle, Michael took her arm and steered her to the parking lot at the side of the restaurant. When Nikki tried to pull back, his grip tightened. She wanted to fight, but she was too tired. By the time they got to his car, she was tired enough to let Jack the Ripper drive her home. The whole evening was a bad dream. She couldn't see straight, couldn't talk without mumbling, and worst of all, she couldn't think. She figured out one thing. Michael was right; she should not be driving. She could barely keep her eyes open.

Michael slipped a key into the passenger lock of a silver Jaguar. When he opened the door, she slid into the seat without argument. She was rubbing her upper arm by the time he got into the driver's seat.

"I'm sorry. Did I hurt you?"

She put her arm down but refused to look at him. "It doesn't matter." She gave him her address and rolled down the window. The evening air was frigid, and just what she needed to revive her depleted energy.

"Are you all right?" he asked, giving her a curious sidelong glance.

"Fine."

"You're sure?"

"I'm sure. Just drive—please." Nikki was determined to avoid all conversation until her head was working properly again. Besides, she was at a loss as to what to say. She was sure someone owed someone an apology, but she couldn't decide who exactly owed whom. Confused thoughts flapped around her brain like a flock of disturbed sparrows. She breathed in the cold night air and shook her head against the insistent lethargy. *Damn. Damn. Damn,* she sputtered, undirected anger tightening her chest like a spastic fist. *What a hash! All I want to do is get home, take off these stupid clothes, shower, and go to bed. I'll figure out what went wrong tomorrow.*

Michael drove in silence until they reached her apartment and he'd parked the car. By the time he reached her side, she was already out the door. She'd taken a determined but wobbly step forward when one of her high heels drilled into the rain-softened earth. When she started to fall, Michael instinctively reached for her.

The second Nikki fell against the warm wall of his chest, she reacted, using him as the focus for her frustrated anger and disappointment. She shoved him away violently as if his touch repulsed her, his very closeness offended her.

"Don't! Get away from me! And stop—stop mauling me!" She spit the words at him. Lifting her eyes to his, she gave him a cruel, stubborn stare and pushed against his chest. She stumbled from his arms, her breath coming in rapid, uneven pants.

Michael recoiled as if struck. She saw the hurt in his eyes and the flare of anger that quickly veiled it. Oh, God, what had she done? She closed her eyes and let out a long, aching breath.

"I'm sorry," she whispered. "I didn't mean that." Now, aside from feeling like a top that just stopped spinning, she felt guilty. "I wasn't thinking and—"

He cut her off. "That's okay. Which way to your place?"

Nikki was going to say she could manage on her own, but thought better of it. "Over there." She pointed to the third door on their left.

Michael took her arm and started toward the door. When they got there, Nikki again rustled in her bag for her keys. When she found them, he took them from her, opened the door, and handed them back.

"You should be fine from here. Good night. You've given me an evening to remember. I'll see you Monday." He started to walk away.

"Michael." She was calling him back. She couldn't believe it.

He turned at the sound of her voice but didn't speak.

"Would you like a cup of coffee?" *What am I doing?* her little voice was screaming in her ear. *Let*

*him go. He's hurt, angry, and disgusted with you. Isn't
that what you wanted?*

Michael ran a hand through his dark hair, thought
for a second, then shook his head. "I don't think so.
I think there's been enough damage inflicted on both
of us tonight. I don't think I have the stamina for another round. Thanks, anyway." He started to turn away
again.

"Please. No battles. Just a cup of coffee. I
promise."

"Tell me then. Is the offer of coffee an attempt to
placate your boss or the man?" He remained standing
a few steps away from her. Under the porch light, she
could see his eyes searching hers.

Nikki knew more than sharing a cup of coffee hinged
on her answer. "The man," she said quietly. "Now
please come in before I pass out in my own doorway."
She forced a smile.

He hesitated again, then moved toward her. Nikki
sighed in relief as he followed her through the door.

"Make yourself comfortable." She took his jacket
and pointed to the leather sofa in her small living room.
"I'll only be a minute."

In her bedroom, she glanced quickly in the mirror
and grimaced at her reflection.

"Yuck," she said aloud, rubbing at a smudge of
blue shadow on her cheek. She was a mess. Quickly,
she tore off her clothes, made a beeline for her tooth-
brush and then the shower. She didn't want to make
him wait, but this was an emergency.

An edgy Michael paced the living room. When he
heard the sound of the shower, he relaxed. Knowing
he had a few minutes to himself before she came back,
he looked around the room.

Nikki's apartment, like the woman herself, had élan.
A style that eschewed rules in favor of personality. It

was color and comfort. On one wall there was a pair of bright prints depicting children playing on the beach. Another wall was covered in travel posters and framed photographs. The remaining wall was bookshelves. He moved toward it.

The books were in no order, suggesting they were read according to mood, not plan. There was William Blake opposite Peter Drucker, a romance novel balanced against an anthology of English literature, and a *Farmer's Almanac* snuggled among Durant's multivolume *Story of Civilization*. The happy chaos of the books made him smile. His own bookshelves looked much the same.

He was scanning a copy of a recent thriller when he heard Nikki come back in the room.

"I'm sorry I took so long. I *had* to shower. It was almost a matter of life and death. I'll make that coffee now."

Michael put the book away and turned to look at her. He said nothing.

She suddenly felt awkward. His eyes made her nervous. She had watched those same eyes for days now. Intelligent, observant, and occasionally hard, they mesmerized her, the emotion in them always openly expressed. Looking at her now, Michael's gaze was honest, a naked display of desire, direct and arousing. Her own response came from a nether place within her. When a sad—regretful—smile crossed Michael's face, the hold was broken. He turned back to the bookshelves. Nikki escaped behind the long bar separating the kitchen from the living room.

She was perfect, Michael thought. Form-fitting denims, blue cotton T-shirt, the blazing fall of hair, all of it was pure, unadorned Nikki. He wondered why she chose to wear a T-shirt with the words GO FOR IT emblazoned across the front. The words were not meant for him, she'd made that plain.

Michael's earlier uncertainties about having coffee with Nikki intensified tenfold now. He was in dangerous territory in this apartment. The confined space between them was electric. He struggled to ignore the current. *Damn it! How can she deny what we both feel? Forget it,* he said to himself, remembering the rough force of her hands pushing against his chest. Her rejection was total. The lady said no with a capital N.

Nicole reached up to the second shelf for the coffee as Michael came up beside her. Without comment, he grasped her outstretched arm and pulled it down, touching it above the elbow.

"Did I do that?" He was looking at the pale beginning of a bruise. "I was rough on you. I'm sorry." He stroked the bruise gently, and cursed himself silently. Bloody Neanderthal thing to do!

"You were right not to let me drive. I don't know what I was thinking. As for the bruise, it's nothing. I bruise if someone gives me a dirty look." She reclaimed her arm and reached again for the coffee. Concentrating on the simple task at hand, she worked to ignore Michael's scrutiny.

"Shall we sit down? The coffee will take a minute or so." Jumpy and unsettled, Nikki headed back to the living room. *Maybe I'm not over my wine fest yet,* she thought. Or maybe it was Michael's continued silence as he followed her, then joined her on the sofa, he at one end, she at the other. One soft leather cushion was empty between them. He fixed his eyes on her and kept them there.

"Nikki, why am I here?"

She fought the impulse to give a glib answer. Why had she asked him in? Nothing had changed. He was still her boss. It was probably the worst decision she'd ever made, and yet sitting here with him across from her, she didn't regret it. She'd never wanted to be with a man so much in her life. He was a beckoning adventure, an unknown road, a exciting mystery waiting to be solved. He was everything she *never* planned for, and she was fascinated with him.

"Nikki?" he prompted, giving her a puzzled glance.

"I want to, uh, apologize," she stammered. "I acted like a common, garden-variety bitch. About tonight . . . dinner . . . can you ever forget it?"

"I'm not sure I want to. I haven't had an evening so memorable for a long time." A hint of his wicked smile returned before his voice deepened. "It was a bravura performance and a hell of a demonstration of what you *think* I wanted from you. Your message was loud and clear."

Michael got up from the sofa and moved to the fireplace. "Shall I light this?" he asked.

"Sure. I'll get the coffee."

Nikki sensed he needed a diversion, and she watched from the kitchen as he fanned a flame to life. When she returned with the coffee, he was leaning against the narrow mantel, his gaze fixed on her as she poured steaming mocha java into two mugs. When he continued to stare at her, she gave him a nervous, puzzled glance.

"I'm wondering if I should apologize, too. If wanting you so bad it aches is some kind of crime. And make no mistake, I do want you." His eyes, intent on her, caught the flame of the fire. "Working with you every day has been a grueling exercise in self-denial. Did you know that? I thought—" He put his coffee mug on the mantel and picked it up again. "Hell, you don't even want to know what I thought. I guess I was counting on my admirable behavior," he smiled at her then, "to make you comfortable about us, make you trust me."

" 'Come into my parlor said the spider to the fly'?" Nikki quoted the words without malice and smiled slightly.

"Something like that."

He went back to sit at his end of the sofa, careful to keep a distance between them. "At work, Nikki, have I made it difficult for you?" he asked.

"No. You've been . . . very nice," she finished lamely.

"Nice." He repeated the word first with a grimace then a slight smile. "I think I prefer the comparison to the spider better." He paused. "What you did tonight, I want you to know—I understand. And while it's hell on the old male ego, don't worry, I *can* take no for an answer."

"I was wrong to do what I did tonight," she broke in. "I thought—" She stopped. "Damn, I don't know what I thought," she finished miserably.

"You thought I was a sex-starved executive with a— what did you call it—leaping libido? You weren't altogether wrong, you know, although I hadn't intended my feelings to appear quite so, uh, trivial."

Nikki's throat constricted and she tried to swallow. He continued.

"It seems I handled it—you—badly, but it doesn't matter now. I leave Wednesday. So let's just say I accept my defeat regretfully but gracefully." He made a move to stand.

"Wednesday! I thought you weren't leaving for two more weeks." *You should be glad, Nikki girl,* she chided herself. *Why this disappointment? He'll be out of your life. From here on in you only have to see him once, maybe twice, a year. You can concentrate on your career.*

Michael relaxed back into the sofa. "Everything is going well. There's no need for me to stay any longer. You're more than capable of handling things from here on. I'll probably be back sometime in the next year, and Darlene will stay for a while. If you have any serious problems, you can always call me. You'll do a great job, Nikki. Prisma is fortunate to have you. You have a solid future with us. In a couple of months, we'll talk about that future in more concrete terms. I think you'll be pleased with what I have to offer you." Michael couched his words in a strictly professional tone. She might as well have been in the office.

"Thanks, Michael," she mumbled. "I'll do my best for you. You can count on it." Nikki was struck by the banality of her own words, but couldn't think what else to say.

He placed his half-empty mug on the coffee table and rose to his feet. "Thanks for the coffee. I'm glad you invited me in. It was a good idea to clear the air. I wouldn't have wanted what happened tonight to damage our working relationship."

Nikki nodded silently and stood uncertainly on the other side of the coffee table.

He headed for the door. When he reached it, he stood and looked back at her. Nikki hadn't moved.

"My jacket?" he asked.

"Oh! Right. I think I carried it into the bedroom. I'll get it."

She retrieved his jacket and handed it to him, watching with growing agony as he shrugged it on. He was leaving. He was more than leaving, she could feel it, he was saying goodbye. She stared at him in bewilderment, eyes wide and slightly fevered. They were only inches apart, but the distance yawned like a mile-wide chasm. She couldn't think how to cross it.

Michael gripped the doorknob and hesitated. What

was he seeing in her eyes? Without thinking, he reached up and brushed a stray wisp of hair off her temple. He saw a trace of the wound he had patched at Whistler. He also saw that her eyes were closing.

"Michael." Her voice was scarcely a whisper but it froze his hand on the knob. She opened her eyes and looked into his. "Kiss me, Michael. I'm asking you to kiss me."

He hesitated; then, like a man unchained, he reached for her.

At the first touch of his lips, Nikki gave way to the emotions she had tried to deny. Dear God, how she needed this man. With that admission, her hard-won restraint crumbled, leaving in its stead a growing, uncontrollable excitement. She shuddered into his arms, repeating his name over and over again whenever he gave her time and breath enough to speak. His kiss was fierce, impatient. She couldn't breathe but didn't care; she had Michael. His hands moved from her shoulders down to the soft rounds of her buttocks, and he pulled her tight to the hard swell of his need. She moaned into his mouth.

"I can't take any more of this, Nikki. You're driving me crazy." His voice was a dull growl. "We have to talk." He pushed her away from him and fought for breath. "You have to be sure." His green eyes, now glazed with desire, sought hers.

"I'm sure. Absolutely and positively sure." She leaned against him and practiced breathing. Try as she might, she couldn't remember any of the reasons that had made her hesitate. She simply had to have him. She smiled up into his worried eyes.

"There's only one thing I need an honest answer to," she said teasingly.

"Try me."

"Will you still respect me in the morning?"

Michael gave a soft laugh, but before he answered, his eyes turned thoughtful. "Respect is a given. What you should be asking is, Will I still love you in the morning. That's much more important, don't you think?" He watched for her response.

"Love? We don't need to talk about that. I know I'm not, uh, too experienced about things, but I'm not so dumb I think you have to say I love you to go to bed with me." Nikki had no intention of ruining what was happening between them. He wanted her. She wanted him—burned for him. It was enough. Why heighten expectations with talk of love that would be doomed to failure by distance and a working relationship?

Michael stepped back, his hands dropping to his sides as he did so. "You don't care how I feel about you? Is that it?"

"Of course I care. I'm trying to be realistic. That's all. Why are you so angry? Is this the first time a woman has wanted your body with no strings attached?"

"It's the first time a woman has been so blunt about it. Is that honestly what you want . . . my body with no strings attached? You're willing to go to bed with me, then let me walk out of here as if nothing more had passed between us than a good-night kiss? You could do that?" He tilted his dark head and looked down at her.

"It's an offer most men wouldn't refuse." She was beginning to feel on shaky ground.

"I'm not most men," he stated flatly.

"And I'm not most women. I won't ask for—or give—vows of love when none are required."

"They're required." He gripped her waist and pulled her closer.

"What are you saying?"

"I'm saying I won't give you my body unless you love me." A knowing smile played around Michael's mouth.

"Are you nuts? Men aren't like that."

"Men aren't like what, exactly?" he teased, running his hands up her sides. "Men don't need honest affection? Men don't care who they make love to as long as they make love? Men never pass up an opportunity no matter how questionable? Is that what you're saying?"

"You're trying to tell me none of that is true?"

"No. Sometimes members of my sex do hit some low notes, but some of us occasionally aspire to something higher."

Nikki snorted her reply. "Like you right now, I suppose?"

"Exactly. Why should I satisfy your sexual urges at the expense of my self-respect?"

"You're kidding. You've got to be kidding."

"Nope. Dead serious. You may want me only for my skill in bed—"

"*Skill?* That I wouldn't know, as you are not about to let me find out if you have any," she interrupted, acutely conscious of his broad palms grazing the sides of her breasts.

He went on as though she hadn't spoken. ". . . but I want more than that. I've wanted more since I first saw you battling that mountain. You're such a stubborn little witch, you never gave me the chance to tell you."

"All right. I'm giving you the chance now. Tell me. What do you want from me? It's obviously not my body. You've already turned that down. So, what is it?"

Michael brought his hands to rest quietly on her waist, pulled a little away, and looked down at her. "I want your trust. That before anything. Then I want your love. All of it, with no reservations. I want you to love me fully, completely—the way I love you. I want to be first in your life.'' He lifted her face to his. ''You must know how I feel about you, Nikki. You can't be so blind you don't see how much I love you.'' The intensity of Michael's emotion was in his words and on his face.

She stared at him. ''You're serious,'' she stated in absolute shock.

''Very serious.'' His eyes would not, could not, release her.

Nikki experienced a sharp, involuntary intake of breath. Michael was holding her, Michael loved her! Was it possible what he'd said that night in his hotel room? That neither of them need lose? It wasn't right, she thought, it isn't time for love. What did his love mean? Happiness? A life together? She couldn't answer, nor could she so easily abandon all her reservations, but she did feel the slow growth of a new confidence.

''That's a tall order,'' she finally answered.

''I know, but I won't settle for less. I can't. Not with you.''

I love you. Three short words. Words she had never said before. Words that would change her life forever. She looked into his eyes, to the source of him. His gaze never wavered. He had to be teasing her, he had to be!

''How about if I love you enough for now—for tonight. Will that do?'' Easy banter. She was a master at it. Still, her voice wasn't quite as steady as she'd have liked.

He studied her long and hard. ''I guess it will have to. Right now I'm a little low in the willpower department.'' He stroked a thumb over her lower lip. ''And the trust? What about the trust?''

"Don't get greedy. I'll have to work on that." She gave him a shaky smile.

He smiled back, his curved lips hovering over hers. "We'll work on it together." He intended a light kiss to seal their bargain, but it proved impossible. When the kiss started to deepen, Nikki pushed him from her and looked into the deep green of his eyes.

"Well?" was all she asked.

She grinned at his puzzled look.

"Now can I have your precious body? Maybe experience some of that skill you were bragging about earlier?"

He rewarded her with a slow, seductive smile. "You gave me a dinner I'll never forget. I'll do my best to give you a night to remember. Although it would be easier if we weren't in a doorway."

Nikki slipped off his jacket and took his hand. "Right this way, sir." As she led him to the bedroom, she looked back at him over her shoulder. "And don't forget to bring that leaping libido."

There was little chance of that, he thought as he watched the sway of her hips, but controlling it might be a problem.

Except for the point of light coming from the half-open bathroom door, her bedroom was dark. Michael glanced around the room only long enough to locate the bed, a bed swathed in pure white linen with a cache of odd-shaped cushions at its head. His eyes turned back to her, and he smiled as she needlessly closed the door behind them. She was nervous, he thought.

Nikki had used up all her bravado to get this far. When they reached the bedroom, she started to panic. She had never had a man in her bedroom before, and the strangeness of it made her tense. What she wanted more than anything was for Michael to take her in his arms again. Everything was all right when he held her.

Recognizing her need, he reached for her, pulling her close against him as though he would never release her. She could feel the potency of his arousal, yet he held her gently, letting his desire warm her, ready her for what she knew would come. A quickening in her own body put her fears to rest, and she tried to move closer, surprised to find her hips pressing against him.

"Just a minute." Michael took a breath and held her from him. Turning her around, he removed the silken loop holding her hair. His fingers coursed their way through its length, separating, then spraying the strands across her back.

His hands grasped her shoulders to pull her back to his chest, and he whispered through the mane of hair, "I've wanted to do that since I found you."

The honesty of his desire bolstered her courage and she turned to face him. "There are a few things I've wanted to do to you, too."

He cocked a questioning brow and grinned.

Nikki studied him for a moment as though looking at a banquet and not quite knowing where to start.

"You're going to have to help."

"Name it." He smiled down at her.

"We could start with the sweater. It has to go."

Michael peeled off the black cashmere in one clean stroke and dropped it at his feet.

"Done. Anything else?"

"I'll take it from here." Nikki had never been so bold with a man. She wanted to be bold, wanted to be free of inhibitions and fears. More than anything she wanted to be an equal, giving partner in this act of love.

Nikki moved back to him and ran her hands across the soft cotton shirt that covered his chest, then down to where it met the waistband of his slacks. She undid his belt and the button on his slacks and pulled his shirt free. She unbuttoned his shirt from the bottom up, pausing occasionally to run her hands over his tight, hard midriff. Only when she undid the last button and pushed the shirt from his shoulders did she look up and into his eyes, letting her hands roam and explore his taut muscles. His chest was wider, more powerful than she expected.

She ran her hands flat through the curling hair on his chest, feeling it spring and wrap around her fingers. She touched one then the other of his smooth male nipples. They stiffened under her touch and she kissed them. She felt Michael's chest heave, quiver slightly, as he took a step back.

His voice was hoarse when he spoke. "I think you're stealing my moves. How about I have a turn now? I've been wanting to do what your T-shirt says to do all night."

Michael didn't wait for her answer. In one fluid motion Nikki's T-shirt joined his cashmere on the floor. He eyed her satin bra, then ran a warm, curious finger under its lace edging before relegating it to the growing pile on the floor.

His emerald eyes stayed on her breasts as he cupped each one fully in his hand. "More perfect than I imagined."

His thumbs teased her nipples, rubbing until they peaked and burned. A soft moan broke through Nikki's lips and her head went back, then rolled to her shoulder. When he heard her moan, Michael bent his head and curled his tongue around each erect, hardened peak. Another, deeper moan escaped, and she pressed his head to her breast, twisting her hands through his thick silky hair.

With a fierce movement, Michael crushed her to him,

then lifted her into his arms. In seconds they were on the bed tangled in each other's arms. Nikki had never felt such need. She was exploding with it, demanding a satisfaction she didn't believe possible. Her breasts were pinned against the hot flesh of Michael's chest and still she wanted closer, then closer again.

With noticeable effort, he leaned away from her and propped himself on one elbow.

"Nikki . . ." He trailed a shaking finger from her lips downward. "You're magnificent. Every part of me aches for you."

She twisted to his hand, breath coming in short uneven gasps. She reached up to pull him back.

"Easy, darling, easy. We have lots of time." Michael was determined to slow down. He wanted his hands and body to show his love, surely, carefully. He wanted her to have no doubt of it. To do that he had to control his own hunger.

He kissed each breast softly, then took one stiffened nipple in his mouth to draw on as his hand moved down the flat plains of her midriff. He let it rest there, his mouth continuing to suckle. When she groaned under him, his hand moved down to the tight waistband of her jeans. The tips of his fingers slipped under it, exploring, sensing. Nikki's breathing stopped when he started to pull down her zipper, then started again when the job was done. He caressed the newly exposed skin with his heated palm, then lifted his head from her aching, thrusting breast. His hand slid down under the silk of her panties to touch the softness between her thighs. He cupped it, then looked into her eyes as he pulled his hand back, one finger stroking silkily through the core of her womanhood. His finger was a torch, and Nikki burned and gasped for air. Suddenly it was critical that she be free of the confining denim. Wriggling against him, she lifted her hips.

"You want me to take them off, Nikki? Is that what you want?" He looked down at her, his verdant eyes dark and possessive.

"Yes." She couldn't think of anything she wanted more.

It took both of them to dispose of the clinging denim. When she lay before him, naked and vulnerable, his hands and mouth sought all of her. He kissed her mouth, her neck, her breasts, the softness of her stomach. He was reaching the inside of her thighs when she said, "Now you, Michael." She stroked the hard ridge pressed against her leg. "I want to see you, too." Her soft touch galvanized him, but before shedding his slacks, he took out the necessary protection.

"Prepared, huh?" Nikki teased, but she was relieved. This relationship would be complicated enough.

"I stopped on the way to dinner. Does it bother you?" He caressed her bare shoulder and tried to gauge her reaction.

"No." Nikki thought a moment. "But how did you know that I would . . . we would . . . ?" She couldn't finish.

"I didn't." He pulled her to him now, and she sensed his smile. "I was counting on my Irish luck."

When the bare sleekness of him covered her, she closed her eyes and molded herself to the contours of his hard male body. The naked strength of his arousal, the sheer power of it, crazed her, softened her, melted her. He rained her body with hot, lingering kisses and she pulsed against him. She felt him struggle for control while her own frenzy was past governing. She was his.

"You feel so good," he whispered. "Warm silk. Perfect. God, how I've wanted you—needed you." He kissed her again—hard—then lifted his head.

Nikki looked into his hungry eyes. The taut ridge of his erection throbbed against her, and she arched into him, gasping her reply. "And I need you. I've never needed anyone like I need you."

"Now?" Michael's hand again slid downward across the curve of her abdomen to her female center. He moved sensuous fingers through its slick moisture, probing into the throbbing heat he found there.

Nikki groaned and dug her nails into the flesh of his shoulders. He was taking her high, showing her greater satisfaction than she'd ever known. A pounding, merciless ache built within her as she luxuriated in the play of his hand on the most secret part of her womanhood. She could bear it no more.

"Now," she moaned, stroking him, opening herself for their pleasure. "Now, Michael." Her low cry was urgent. She didn't know what was happening to her. It was so good, he was so good.

At the touch of her hand, the sound of her voice, a hoarse growl tore loose from his throat and he swung himself between her open thighs. With a swift, sure movement, he entered her. Deeply. Fully. Nikki cried out to ease pleasure's ache.

Mindful of his strength, Michael held back, rotated his hips, controlled his thrust. She was small. Slowly, he began to move, his male rhythm sure, powerful, and commanding. Nikki clung to him, sensation after sensation breaking over her, unknown muscles deep within her flexing and tensing. Together they reached for, demanded, the fierce intensity of release. It came. Full and primal. An ecstasy of senses. At once emptying and leaving them full. Nikki cried out with the sheer joy of it as Michael pulled her to his heart.

Neither of them spoke for the time it took for breath and reality to filter back. Nikki had the feeling she was returning from a long journey. A journey of delight, she thought, shifting under the weight of Michael's body, a body still hot and damp from lovemaking. He lifted his head, looked down at her, then rolled off to her side. She shivered at the loss of his body heat, and he drew her to him. He kissed her forehead and smoothed the damp tendrils of her hair from her face.

She curled into him, her face in the curve of his throat. Savoring the feel of him, she warmed herself in the lingering heat of their lovemaking. She was sated, happy. She wanted to extend this moment. Could she believe he wanted that, too? He wanted her trust, but she couldn't risk that. *Keep it light, Nikki, and keep it distant*, she told herself. Light and distant—now those were words she recognized; those were words to trust.

"Are you cold?" he asked.

"No. I'm perfect. Just perfect," she purred.

"That I already know." He ran his fingers through her hair. "That's why I love you."

"Do you know what we need?" The question was mumbled into his shoulder.

"I think we just had it, but if you give me a minute or two . . ."

Nikki pushed herself away from him and smiled into his eyes. "Besides that."

"I didn't know there was a *besides*." He touched her lower lip with his thumb, and rubbed it softly.

"We need two cigarettes. You should be lighting them, one for me, and one for you. I always wanted to do that."

"That's a bit of a problem, isn't it, considering neither of us smoke?"

"True. But think about it. Right now we could both be lying back in a sexy blue haze, staring at the ceiling, each of us lost in our own thoughts. You have to admit smoking has a way of filling up awkward moments."

"Do you feel awkward, Nikki?" He turned the full force of his green eyes to her face.

"Maybe . . . a little. It's not everyday I go to bed

with my boss, you know.'' She pulled away from him.
''To be honest, it's not everyday I go to bed with
anyone.''

''I know.''

''That obvious, huh?'' Nikki wished she'd kept her
mouth shut. She was embarrassed now. Had she been
so inept? She'd be damned if she'd ask. She lifted her
chin a notch and tried to get up, dragging the rumpled
sheet around her nakedness.

''Come back here.'' He wouldn't let her go. ''What
was obvious was a lot of pent-up emotion and a woman
brimming with passion—fire—and precious little patience. It was wonderful; you were wonderful. If I
hadn't been in such a hurry myself . . .'' His words
ended in a line of feathery kisses starting at the base
of her throat and ending at her lips. He brought her
closer, and his mouth hovered over hers. ''In one fell
swoop, you completely restored my damaged male ego.
For that I'll be eternally grateful.'' He kissed her softly
then and pulled away the twisted sheet. ''As for awkward moments, I have a suggestion.'' He continued the
slow torture of his caresses.

Nikki's mouth was dry. She felt herself slipping
away again, lost in the dark, shadowy jade of his eyes,
lulled by the low timbre of his voice. She could
scarcely speak. She couldn't speak. She could only
feel.

''Uh huh?'' was the best she could do. His hand was
on her breast now, stroking a tender nipple, his mouth
spilling erotic, whispered kisses into her ear. She was
losing her ability to breathe. Suddenly, he shuddered
and pulled away. She could see he was shaking.

''Damn!'' he muttered to himself.

''What's the matter?'' His sudden fierceness alarmed
her.

''You. You're what's the matter. I want to slow

down, Nikki. I want to please you, but when I touch you I get so hot it's impossible. The second time should be better—long and slow.'' He traced her face with an unsure hand. ''If I keep up this pace, I'm going to confirm your worst suspicions about me.''

Nikki gave him a slow smile, and for a moment, relished the power she had over him.

''Why don't we try for long and slow, the third time out? For now, let's just . . . go for it!''

_____ FOURTEEN _____

When Nikki opened her eyes the next morning, it was only six-thirty. On a Saturday morning that time required no action, so she burrowed back into the bed. She was vaguely aware her movements were hampered, that she was cocooned in a sheet. The front of her was warm, but her back was freezing. The twist of sheet barely covered her buttocks. She groped for her goose down comforter but found Michael's muscular thigh instead. The night came back in a rush, and Nikki reddened at the thought of what they'd shared—and how often! There were strange new feelings to sort out, but not now. Now she could only stare at the man in her bed. She eased herself up on one elbow for a better view.

He had asked her if she wanted him to leave. She remembered that, and she remembered, too, asking him to stay. Now she wondered if that was such a good idea. Surely it would have been easier to wake up alone, easier to avoid the morning after. _Whatever am I going to say to him? Whatever is he going to say to me?_

Michael was sleeping on his stomach, one leg bent at the knee. His black hair was mussed against her white pillow. The contrast was startling. He was disturbingly handsome, she thought as she studied the side of his face that was visible. For the first time she noticed a pale, thin scar above his left eye. It was parallel to the line of his brow. It was the only imperfection she could see.

Except for the part of him her body rested against, he must be cold, she thought. She never turned the heat on in her bedroom. She groped for the comforter to cover him. It was at the bottom of the bed, and she had to lift herself away from him to reach for it. His response was immediate. He turned toward her and opened his eyes. His hand reached out and stroked her upper arm.

"Hi." He was unconcerned with his nakedness. He should be, she told herself. His body was bloody perfect.

"Hi," she stammered back, grabbing for the rumpled quilt.

"What are you doing?"

"Trying to find a cover."

"Come here. If you're cold, I'll warm you."

"No, it's not me . . . it's you. I thought you might be chilly." Nikki voice sounded strange, even to herself.

He let her go then, raised himself on one elbow, and watched her. "Awkward moment again?"

"No. It's just that . . . well—"

Michael didn't want her to feel uncomfortable, but it was obvious she did. Her face was flushed, and she couldn't meet his eyes. He wanted to pull her to him, make her talk about what was bothering her, but something told him it was the wrong thing to do. What she needed now was space. He knew instinctively she needed to reflect on what had happened between them. *So do I, for that matter,* he thought. *Although maybe for different reasons.*

She tugged at the comforter, stuck somewhere between the mattress and the footboard. Michael watched. *You love me, Nicole Johnson,* he said to himself. *You just haven't figured out how much or how this unplanned emotion is going to fit into your life—or your career.* A shot of fear pierced him. Would she push him away again? She freed the quilt, then fussed with it, pulling it up and over them. She was careful to keep a distance between them. Yes, definitely space, he thought again. But not too much space.

Michael shifted his body weight fully to his side, and placed a warm hand on Nikki's throat. His thumb rested on its pulse. He could feel it quicken. He grazed her mouth with a light kiss and lifted his head to look at her.

"How would you like to go skiing?"

"Skiing! What ever made you think of that?" She hadn't expected this. Michael had read her correctly, though. Nikki did want breathing room and some physical outlet.

"I thought it would be a good idea to return to the scene of the crime. The place I first fell in love with you." He smiled at her.

Michael noticed the cloud of disbelief that crossed her face when he mentioned love but let it pass. *Is it me you don't trust,* he wondered, *or yourself?* One thing was certain: the morning had brought with it seeds of doubt. No way would he let them take root.

"The cabin is sitting empty. Why not use it? Everything I need is already there, and it won't take long for you to get your gear together. If we leave now, we can have breakfast on the way and be on the slopes by ten-thirty or so. What do you say?" He stroked her shoulder and upper arm with a careful casualness. "We can ski today and tomorrow and be back tomorrow night."

"I don't know . . ." Nikki didn't know. She found it impossible to sort out her feelings. She still couldn't believe she was in her own bed naked beside her boss. It was insane, and what was more insane was how she felt about him.

She loved him. She couldn't believe it! She actually loved him. But she wasn't ready for love, and she sure wasn't ready for loving Michael Dorado. She had goals, ambitions, worlds to conquer before she even considered falling in love. She needed to prove herself.

While the thought of going back to Whistler was appealing, she wasn't sure it would be smart to spend another night with him. She was at the brink now. Another night like last night and she'd be over it. Downstream without a canoe. *Be honest, Nicole Johnson, it isn't the sleeping part that bothers you.* Even the casual touch of his hand on her shoulder was inflaming her, raising her body heat.

As if he were reading her mind, he said, "No strings attached, Nikki. There are three bedrooms in the cabin, and we both could use time to think. There's no better place to do it. Not to mention that the skiing will be great."

Keep it light, Nicole, she said to herself again. "You mean you won't kiss me unless I ask you to?" she tried to tease.

Michael appeared to give it thought, and then the straight line of his mouth curved into a mischievous smile. "I don't think I can promise not to kiss you. We have, it seems, gone quite a bit past that." He raised his right hand. "But I give you my Boy Scout promise to respect your wishes about whether or not we go beyond that. Fair enough?"

"You were a Boy Scout?" Nikki raised a disbelieving eyebrow.

"Of course." He gave her an innocent smile, rolled to his side of the bed, and put his feet on the floor. When he turned back to her, he was still smiling. "Time to start building that trust, Nikki. What do you say?"

There was only one thing to do. Smile back. "Okay, but I'm first in the shower."

"We could save time and water if we showered together. Maybe help the environment?" he suggested gravely, then raised both hands at the look in her eye. "Okay, okay. You shower. I'll make coffee."

Michael had been right, Nikki decided within minutes of arriving back at Whistler. It was exactly the place to be. There was fresh snow on the mountain and a brilliant winter sun. The lifts were busy, but the wait was minimal. Within half an hour, they were standing at the top of Blackcomb. As she stood beside him, she was again captivated by the endless view. It always amazed her how so few of the skiers ever stopped to look. They shot up the mountain on the high-speed lifts and then down as fast as their technically advanced skis could take them. What a waste, she thought. Michael felt the same.

"You know, I think this view is what the word magnificent was coined for," he said.

Nikki didn't answer right away. She was scanning the peaks of the surrounding mountains, rapt in their towering beauty. "Someone once said that great things can happen when men and mountains meet. What do you think?"

"I think he was right. I know I already owe this mountain a debt. Where else would I have met an otherwise sophisticated businesswoman wearing the most godawful hat I've ever seen.''

Nikki suppressed a giggle. "It did make a statement.''

"Yes, it did." He smiled down at her, his height accentuated by the ski boots and the black ski outfit. A black relieved only by a single flash of neon lightning down the back of his jacket. "Now, how about we accomplish some great things on this slope. Do you think Cougar Chute qualifies? Or is that a problem for you?" he goaded.

She flashed him a wicked smile. "It definitely qualifies, and the only problem will be you—keeping up with me. Ready?''

Michael pulled down his goggles and spiked the snow with his poles. "Ready. Let's do it."

By the time Nikki and Michael reached the cabin, daylight was fading. They were both exhausted and locked in a no-win argument about who was first down on the last run. They had skied hard, exercised to their physical limits, and laughed continually. Nikki had seen evidence of Michael's wit over the past couple of weeks, but nothing like today.

The relaxed man she'd been flying down the mountain with since morning was good-natured and quick to laugh, as much at himself as anyone else. She delighted in his sense of humor, feeling as though she'd uncovered a hidden treasure. It was obvious that Michael shared her love of activity and competition. And, like her, he didn't give an inch if he thought he was ahead in the game. At least not an inch she could see.

Nikki collapsed on the bench, the same bench she had sat on so tentatively just days ago. Now, like then, Michael bent over her to help her off with her boots. She leaned her head back and closed her eyes.

"I'm zonked. You may have to carry me up the stairs. Better yet, maybe I'll put my head down right here and you can wake me in the morning."

Michael was sitting beside her now, taking off his own boots. "Don't pull that frail female routine on me. After today it won't wash. Come on. On your feet. I have just enough energy left to light a fire and scare up dinner. Please say you don't want to go out."

"No. I don't want to go out. I'll eat a can of cold beans to avoid that, but first I want a pounding hot shower." Michael took her hand and pulled her upright. He gave her a quick affectionate hug, took her hand, and led her up the stairs.

"I think we can do better than a can of beans. As for the shower, there's something here that will do a lot more for those skied-out muscles. I'll show you."

He led her to a door that looked like it would lead outside. Instead it led to an atrium dominated by a large Jacuzzi tub. The glass room was filled with steam. He opened a window vent and flicked a switch on the wall. The water boiled to life with an inviting froth.

"This will perform miracles, and give you an appetite for whatever I can find in the fridge."

Nikki stared at the tub. Never had water looked so inviting. *If I don't go in there,* she thought, *my muscles will never forgive me.* But there was no mistaking the tub was meant for two. Did she dare? She looked at the handsome man at her side. One quick glance and it felt like a fist had closed around her heart. She thought about last night, the strength and purpose of his body, how it had delighted her. A curious knot formed in her stomach. She knew there would be no relief for it unless . . .

"What about your appetite? Doesn't it need help, too?"

"Are you saying what I think you're saying?" The

look of surprise on his face was genuine. He had promised himself not to push it, to take it easy. Wasn't that what she wanted? Would he ever understand this woman? Somehow he hoped not.

"I'm trying to say that this here tub . . ." she placed a ski-socked toe on its edge, "is meant for two. Now where is that shower?"

Michael smiled and took her hand. "This way, pretty lady. And this time we conserve water."

After their shower, Michael left Nikki combing her hair and went to check the water temperature. Deciding it was perfect, he dropped the towel he'd draped around his lean waist and settled into the frothing water. A hot tub was a strange place to come to cool down, he thought, but that was exactly what he intended to do.

He took a breath and stretched his arms back across the rim of the tub. He'd barely managed not to seduce her in the shower, and his blood was fevered. He'd never met a woman who had such an immediate and startling effect on his passions. *I always considered myself a controlled kind of guy,* he thought. *That's a laugh.*

Thinking about the day they had shared, he smiled. There were no halfway measures with Nikki, he decided. She gave everything her best shot whether it was sport, business, or, as he happily discovered last night, lovemaking. He remembered again thinking she was just a sassy teenager that first day on the mountain. *I was half right,* he grinned to himself.

He loved her. Hell, he was mad for her. And he had no doubts, none at all, but he was uncertain of her. Her own words of love were reluctant, timorous. He sensed her conflict, but was unsure of its root. There was always busywork going on in that head of hers, a sorting and shuffling process that kept him on edge. He frowned when he thought maybe she might never be certain enough to fully admit her love. To commit to him.

"That's a strangely worried look for a man who has everything."

He hadn't heard her come in. He looked up and quickly smiled when he saw her standing over him, wrapped in a large towel. Her hair was darkly wet, slicked back severely from her high forehead, and in the misty half-light of the atrium, her skin glowed like warm cream. His eyes wandered over the lean curves of her body and his look turned hungry. He reached out his hand and gave a playful tug on her towel. She smiled and tightened her grip.

"I don't have everything. Not yet." A stronger tug and the towel heaped at her feet. "But I'm getting close."

Nikki wasted no time getting into the tub. Despite the intimacies they'd shared, she still had moments of uneasiness when he so openly scanned her body. She wasn't ashamed of it exactly, but she had no idea how it measured up in his eyes. When he looked at her that way, the way he had in the shower, the way he was looking at her now, she found herself wishing she'd been more zealous about her aerobics classes, wishing her breasts were bigger, wishing her waist was smaller—wishing she was perfect. Still, the fire in his gaze told her she hadn't completely failed the test.

Nikki settled into the tub directly opposite him. He made no move toward her, content to watch her relax and enjoy the surging water.

"This is heaven, absolute heaven." She gave him a languid gaze. "I thank you. My poor body thanks you."

"There's nothing poor about your body. I can attest to that." He smiled at her then. It was an intense, dusky kind of smile that reached her on a special channel. There was no way in the world she could handle what this man did to her. No way at all. Her eyes locked on his now-serious face and she sighed. She wished again he was anybody other than her boss. Her own expression deepened into a worried frown.

"I didn't mean to embarrass you." He totally misread her mood.

"You didn't. It's just when I think about it, about us, it confuses me. Maybe even frightens me. I can't think straight when I'm around you, and if there is one thing I've always been able to do, it's think straight. It's a whole new problem for me."

"You still think what's between us is a problem?"

"Don't you?"

"No. No, I don't. I think what's between us is love."

"How can you be so sure that it's not just . . ."

"Sex?" he finished.

"Yes."

"Because I know. So do you, or you will when you look deep enough."

Nikki gave him a plaintive look. "Maybe I don't want to. Look deep enough, I mean. It's not the right time for me to fall in love. There's my job. I've got so much to do, so much to accomplish."

Michael had heard enough. He pushed a button on the side of the tub to still the water's noisy boil, then crossed to Nikki's side. He took her face between his strong hands and fixed his eyes on her.

"There's only one thing you have to do, and that's decide exactly what's important to your life, the whole of your life. Decide what comes first, the rest of it will follow. I'm selfish enough to want that place for myself." He smiled at her then. "You do love me, you know. I consider that a good start."

Nikki lifted her arms from the now-quiet water and

draped them loosely across his broad, wet shoulders. "You make it sound simple," she sighed. "It's not simple at all. Loving you is exactly what complicates things. Loving you doesn't automatically erase my ambitions, Michael. I have plans for my life. Things I need to prove to myself—and others."

"Who said anything about erasing them? Your ambition is part of you. A part that I admire and respect. It's a question of priorities, Nikki, not abandonment."

He moved closer and the points of her nipples skimmed the dark hair of his chest. Her hands caressed his shoulders. Willing his own hands to slow service, he moved them to her waist and pulled her closer. One hand stroked upward and cupped her breast.

She looked into his eyes and gave him her total attention. "You make everything seem easy. It's not easy, you know. How can you talk about setting priorities at a time like this?"

He kissed her then, long and deep, then moved his dark head to whisper raggedly in her ear, "At the moment, my love, I have no problem with priorities."

She could feel his hands stroking her outer thighs and with that gentle stroke came a directional change in her thinking. *Damn it,* she thought as she pulled him closer. *There goes my logical thinking.* The thought made her sinfully happy. She was even happier when, in a bold move, he removed one of her hands from his shoulders and dragged it under the water, pressing it against the fullness of his arousal. She gasped her pleasure.

One errant thought intruded before Michael's hands worked their magic. A sudden picture of her successful father and brothers. They had such high expectations of her. A look of consternation claimed her face. *What would they think if they could see me now, naked, slick as a newborn, caressing my boss in a hot tub?* Suddenly, she couldn't suppress a giggle.

Michael heard nothing. He was busy. Very busy. And in seconds, so was Nikki.

"Coffee, Niks?" Amy asked as she passed Nikki's open office door. "And how come you're in so late? Starting to keep executive hours already?"

"What do you mean late? It's only eight-fifteen."

"For you that's late. You haven't been in here later than seven-thirty since the Prisma takeover. Busy weekend, maybe? Anything—or anyone—I should know about?" Amy teased innocently.

Nikki instantly reddened, damning for the millionth time the pale skin that so easily betrayed her. Amy didn't miss the blush, and her curiosity flared. She was about to ask some probing questions when Christy arrived unannounced carrying two coffees. She took a seat opposite Nikki's desk and pushed one of the coffees toward her. She was settling in.

Nikki groaned inwardly. She wasn't ready for this. And Christy's opening comments didn't help.

"You're doing a pretty good imitation of a boiled lobster, Nikki. What's up?" Christy's words were as breezy as usual, but Nikki could feel the interest in her gaze.

"Exactly what I was asking," Amy chimed in. "Come on, Niks, fill us in."

"Can you guys give me a break? It's too early to exchange confidences. Even if I had any. Which I don't," she added quickly.

"Aha!" Christy snorted. "She's falling back on executive privilege, Amy. Doesn't think we mere working stiffs will appreciate the lifestyle of the newly rich and famous. Tell us, Nikki, do general managers really have more fun?"

Nikki couldn't help but laugh. She also couldn't help the increasing redness of her skin.

"If you must know, I went skiing."

"Yes . . . ?" Christy and Amy chimed in unison.

"And I didn't get home until late. I probably got a little too much sun and wind. Does that satisfy your totally unjustified curiosity?" She was dreading it, but she knew they were going to ask if she went alone, and she prepared herself to lie. She didn't want to; she had to. The alternative was to set the office buzzing about her and Michael. Nikki couldn't bear that. She hated liars, hated lying even more. She felt trapped, frustrated, and then angry.

She didn't hear Michael come into her office through the adjoining door. The sound of his voice added to her discomfort.

"Ski weekends can be exhausting, Nikki, but I hope you're not too tired to make sense out of these production statistics. They came in this morning." His voice was perfectly level, as though this was just another day at the office. He was holding computer printouts. He smiled a good morning to Christy and Amy.

"I hate to break up your meeting." He raised the printouts and shrugged his shoulders. "But do you mind if I steal Nikki for a moment before Darlene gets here? I've got a lot to do before Wednesday."

"Can I ask you one quick question, Michael?" Amy asked.

"Sure. What is it?"

Nikki tuned out of the conversation. She was grateful for his rescue from her curious friends, but she was also furious. His easy coolness enraged her, not to mention the casual reminder that he was leaving Wednesday. Somehow, among all the things they talked about over the weekend, that fact wasn't discussed. *You could have brought it up, Nikki,* she said to herself, *but you avoided it. Yes, but damn it, so did he—until now.*

She was at war with herself now. His words of love were at odds with the reality of a jet leaving day after tomorrow. *Get real,* she told herself. *Did you expect him to change his plans?* Her next thought was, *So this is what an office affair is like.* This was the morning after when cold truth brushed away the moonbeams and stardust. The reality was harsh, she discovered, very harsh. *I've been a fool,* she moaned, *a jackass and a fool.* She knew he was looking at her, but for now, she couldn't bring herself to meet his eyes. Instead she shuffled papers on her desk, moving them first here and then there.

I knew when I got up for work this morning, things would be different. I didn't know how different. She thought about Friday afternoon. Her intentions, when she'd begun her charade and invited Michael out to dinner, now made her laugh. It had been a serious mistake, a major backfire.

Nikki was a stew of emotions: anger, uncertainty, frustration, and yes, shame. She didn't like hiding from her friends, as though she were keeping some dirty little secret, but she had no idea what to do about it. She glanced up at Michael. His conversation with Amy was over, and he was smiling at the two women about to leave her office. Briefly, he returned her gaze and his eyes softened. Was it understanding she saw in his eyes? How could she tell?

Amy looked at both of them before speaking. ''Okay, we're history. Let's go, Christy.'' She sensed the tension in the room.

''But we'll be back, Nikki. So be prepared to tell us all,'' Christy teased as she left the room.

Nikki gave them a weak smile as they left. Her face was ashen now.

"You okay?" Michael was openly concerned now. "I guess this is difficult for you."

"A little." Nikki's tone was curt.

"I'm sorry, but—"

She cut him off. She was an ice woman—unyielding posture, cold eyes, and frigid words. "Look, don't worry about it. I'm a big girl. I'll handle it. After all, it goes with the territory, doesn't it."

He looked genuinely confused. "Territory?"

"Office nymph. Bimbo. Whatever the current label is."

"For God's sake, Nikki!" He made a move toward her. "You can't think that I—"

He was interrupted midstride by the entrance of Darlene. "Good morning, every—" She felt the vibrations and broke off. "Uh, shall I come back later?" She glanced nervously at her watch. "I *am* a bit early. If you two have something you're working on . . ."

"No. You're not too early, Darlene." Nikki's voice was coldly stubborn when she raised her eyes to Michael. His own looked shellshocked. "We were working on something, but it's done. Over. And I hope to Mr. Dorado's complete satisfaction. He's all yours, Darlene. I know he has a lot to do before he leaves." Her eyes fixed on his, she asked, "You did say Wednesday, didn't you?"

Michael stared at her for a long moment as if she were a stranger. She stared back, her face rigid with purpose. His own face settled into a pained, angry mask, and his tone was brusque when he answered, "That's right. Wednesday. None too soon for some people, I can see. Come in, Darlene. Let's get started. We don't want to take up any more of Nikki's valuable time."

Michael strode to the boardroom and a thoroughly confused Darlene followed.

* * *

Nikki avoided being alone with Michael all that day. She had to admit he made it easy. He neither sought her out nor made any effort to bridge the uneasy space between them. They continued the pattern of working together that had developed over the past couple of weeks, concentrating their efforts on the day's agenda. The weekend was erased. If a look or touch threatened to bring it back, Nikki ignored it. She assumed Michael did, too.

The business of Prisma continued. The romance was over. There was no red rose that day, and if Nikki guessed correctly, there would be none tomorrow. She glanced at the velvet crimson of Friday's flower. It was already wilted; three of its leaves, curled and dry, lay on her desk, the whisper of its passion spent and silent.

When Michael asked her to stay later and work on the promotional material for the Belleza products, she declined, claiming a headache. He started to say something then but stopped. Nikki saw the tensing of a tiny muscle near his jaw, the confusion in his eyes, and turned away.

She couldn't risk being alone with him now, at the end of the day. She might weaken. As the day had gone on, her frustration and anger had started to dissipate. She still wished the weekend had never happened, but she couldn't stem the rush of wild emotions that rendered her senseless when she was close to Michael. More than once she jumped away from him when that closeness threatened to bring their bodies in contact.

It was five o'clock. Nikki finished keying a brief memo, put it in the print queue for tomorrow, and switched off the machine. She leaned back in her chair and rubbed her forehead. Damn it! She was getting a headache. *Serves you right for lying,* she thought ruefully. Oh, well, she had the whole evening ahead to nurse it with no interruptions. A quick tidy of her desk surface, and she was at her door, donning her coat. She looked back at the door separating her office from the boardroom where she knew Michael was still working. She was tempted to open it, poke her head in, and say good night. After all, she'd done that routinely every night for the past couple of weeks. *This is not a routine night,* she reminded herself. She opened her office door and slipped out, closing it firmly behind her.

Michael heard the door close. At the sound of Nikki's hurried steps past the boardroom, he let out a long breath and threw down his pen. He ran both hands through his black hair and stood. He started to pace, then stopped at the window facing the view of the inlet. The lights of Vancouver glittered across its width, but he didn't see them. Damn the woman and damn him for being all kinds of fool. He let out a harsh breath, wishing to hell he could call back the cold, power-giving anger of this morning. All he could feel was frustration. Impotence. He relished neither.

If she'd just given him a chance, he would have asked her— Abruptly he resumed pacing.

To hell with it, he thought. He had no use for a woman who didn't know what she wanted or needed, a woman who couldn't tell a sordid office tryst from love. And he sure as hell didn't need an inflexible career woman willing to put love on hold until after her next promotion.

"Michael?"

There was something in the voice. He spun around, hoping. . . .

"Oh. Amy." He tried to cover his disappointment.

"I'm glad you're still here. Have you got a second?"

"I've got more than a second. Sit down." He moved back to the chair he'd just left and motioned her to another across the table.

Amy shook her head at the suggestion of sitting. "I wanted to let you know I heard from Sean today. He'll be here in a few days." Amy was glowing with the news.

"I'm happy for you—and Sean. You must be excited."

He sounded sincere enough, but Amy wondered about the sadness in his eyes.

"Excited doesn't begin to describe it. Scared, too, though. It's been almost two years since we've seen each other." Amy's eyes drifted from Michael as did her thoughts. "I can still see him so clearly in my mind—his blue eyes, the color of his hair, his . . ." She stopped, suddenly embarrassed. "I guess I sound lovestruck, huh?"

"Just a little, but it sounds good. Women wear love well." Most women, he thought before continuing. "Like I said, Sean is a lucky man."

"Yeah, well. I wanted to say thanks—again. It was one lucky day when you decided to buy Kingway."

A grimace of pain passed over Michael's even features. "Yes. Wasn't it though?" Lucky for who? he thought.

Amy moved toward the door. When she reached it, she turned and looked back at the brooding man. He was twisting a pen in his hands with enough force to break it in two.

Amy knew she had no right to interfere; she shouldn't be poking her nose into business that wasn't her concern, but damn it, Nikki *was* her concern. And Michael? Besides being the president, if things went well between Sean and her, he would be family, for heaven's sake. She decided to chance it.

"You shouldn't give up, you know." Amy took a shot in the dark. "Nikki's worth fighting for."

Michael was stunned. Had Nikki talked to Amy about their relationship? He couldn't believe that.

"No. I haven't talked to her, if that's what you're wondering. When Niks is in struggle mode, there's no point in even trying to talk."

"Struggle mode?" he repeated. As he said it, he thought how apt a phrase it was.

"That's what I call it when Nikki is trying to make a decision or change something. She thinks she's one cool lady, but she's not, you know. She's an open book. The chapters might be out of order, and part of it's written in ancient Greek, but everything's there if you know how to read it."

Michael couldn't bring himself to discuss his relationship with Nikki, but he didn't stop Amy when she went on.

"For one thing, she gets terribly fixated. I've never seen anyone so single-minded about setting and working toward goals. From what she tells me, it's something her father taught her. She's so determined at times, it's downright scary. I guess that's good as far as it goes, but Nikki goes wonky when someone drops a monkey wrench into her plans or she has to adjust course. It's not that she's inflexible, she's just a little cautious." Amy looked at Michael then. He remained silent, but there was no mistaking his interest. She plunged on. *Nikki will kill me*, she thought.

"It's like she has set ideas about how things should be, and when there's an unexpected change she—I don't know—overreacts is as good a description as any, I guess. It just takes longer for her to find her balance. You need a lot of patience or . . . you hit her over the head with a hammer." Amy laughed. "Sometimes that does the trick."

Michael was quiet again. A dim light fell across his confusion. He'd thought he understood Nikki, but had he in fact misjudged how strongly focused she could be? And wasn't he much the same way? Like her, he hated to alter a course once it was set upon. To do so took a conscious effort and always left a residue of guilt as if he'd failed somehow, even when the new direction proved to be the better one. It was as though by switching direction he was untrue to himself. Was that how Nikki saw it? Did she see love as some kind of dangerous detour? He heard Amy open the door, then pause.

"I've probably said too much already, Michael, but I do hope you don't give up on Niks. Like I said, she's worth the effort. And about Sean, thanks." She was gone.

Michael rose from his chair and started to pace. *Don't give up. Worth the effort.* Amy's words prodded him on. He frowned. He wasn't at all sure his battered ego was up to another risk. He took a deep breath and for a moment closed his eyes. Nikki's face was before him, every delicate feature etched against his eyelids. "Kiss me, Michael, I'm asking you to kiss me." Her whisper floated to his ear. He started to burn, and his eyelids jerked open.

Hadn't old Coogan always told him, "Don't stop until it's over, me boyo. And only you will know that moment." Well, what was between him and Nikki sure as hell wasn't over. He had to try again. But only once more, he said to himself as he shrugged on his jacket. And he had no intention of being patient.

FIFTEEN

Nikki was wrecked. She kept telling herself she was doing the right thing, but she was wrecked anyway. She hadn't slept last night, or the night before. Gruesome words came to mind. The nights were killing her and the mornings were murder. When she thought about it, she realized she hadn't slept properly since meeting Michael. But that problem would soon be solved. Today, to be exact. The thought of it caused violence in her stomach. Deep in her stomach.

It was Wednesday and he was leaving. Nikki looked again at the memo on her desk. It was from Darlene, reminding her, as if she needed reminding, about his flight plans. His plane was departing Vancouver International at 4:00 P.M. There was a request for reports and data he would need for the Prisma directors in Madrid. Would Nikki make sure he had everything? The memo brought a smile to her lips. The ever-organized Darlene. She'd come to have a solid respect for her these past weeks, not to mention a rather odd but growing affection. *You never know when you'll make a friend,* she thought idly, trying to steer her thoughts away from the man in the next office.

213

She slumped back in her chair and looked at the tiny crystal clock on her desk. Seven twenty-five. Plenty of time to gather the necessary information. She switched on her terminal and did a quick search for the sales figures Darlene had asked for. When she found the file she was looking for, she retrieved it to her screen and prepared to coax the numbers into a solid, useful format. The mass of digits refused to register, and she sat staring blankly at the blink, blink, blink of the cursor. Unable to make sense of it, she pushed her chair back. *Coffee,* she said to herself. *I need coffee.* She pointed herself in the direction of the coffee room.

She couldn't make sense of her thoughts, either. Like the images on her screen, they were at once familiar and alien. At least the numbers on her screen were in neat little rows. Not so her tangled thoughts. They were helter-skelter, beyond interpretation. And Michael? Michael was the cursor, a constant flashing light. It was beyond her willpower to ignore him.

She got her coffee and returned to her desk. On her way, she passed Amy without acknowledgment, didn't even see her. Michael was leaving today. She wouldn't see him for months, maybe never, if he replaced himself by hiring a new president. Never see him again, she thought. That was what she wanted, wasn't it?

Nikki sat back in her chair, feeling slightly ill. Never see Michael again, she repeated, and tried desperately to accept the idea, to adjust to a newer, colder world. A thousand times in the last two days she'd reached for the phone. A thousand times she'd stayed her hand. Michael had given her no opening, steadfastly maintaining his steely, unconcerned composure, a stance that fed all her insecurities. *He's glad,* she told herself, *glad it's over between us. He only wanted a fling anyway.* When she remembered his words of love, and her own, she fought them. It wouldn't work. He didn't mean those words. When she remembered his body, his hands moving over her, touching her where she'd never been touched, she blazed with unbearable fierceness. *Never again,* she vowed. Her very soul ached.

"Definitely struggle mode." Amy was standing in the doorway.

Nikki's eyes fluttered to a reasonable facsimile of sanity. "What?"

"Never mind. Here's that copy of your Whistler presentation you asked for. What do you want it for anyway?"

"I don't want it. Michael does. Darlene says he wants it for reference. He leaves today, you know?" Nikki worked to keep her voice normal.

"I know. So does everyone else in the office. It's not exactly top secret." Amy's voice was flat, impatient. "The question is, what are you going to do about it?" She leveled her eyes to Nikki. Her words were a dare.

"Me? Do? What should *I* do?"

"I wish I could tell you. If you haven't decided yourself by now, I guess it's bye-bye love." Amy started out the door, but not before one final pronouncement. "You know, Nicole Johnson, there are times when you're the biggest jerk I know."

Nikki put her head back and let out a sigh. *You're right, Amy, I am a jerk, but there doesn't seem to be a damn thing I can do about it.* She thought again about the crisp, confident Michael Dorado she had worked with the last two days. The new, improved, totally unapproachable Michael Dorado. He wanted nothing more to do with her, she was sure of it. After all, what man wanted a woman who blew hot one minute and cold the next. How could she expect him to understand? Her blessed career! She fretted about it like it was something that would save the planet. Sure, her work was important to her, it always would be, but not nearly as important as . . . Michael. God, she was going to cry.

Nikki blew her nose, drank some tepid coffee, and dragged herself back to control. Work, Nikki. Do some work. If it can't take the pain away, you know you're in trouble. She turned back to her computer. In fits and starts, she managed to get a few things done. An hour or so later, Darlene showed up.

"Nicole, I wanted to let you know Michael won't be in today. He had a couple of meetings this morning and he's decided to go straight to the airport. He specifically wanted me to give you his respects and gratitude for all your good work. He said you made his stay in Vancouver a most productive one."

Nikki gaped at her, stunned and disbelieving.

"Is something wrong?" Darlene gave her a worried look.

Nikki tried for her voice, but only managed a muffled stammer.

"Nikki?" It was the first time Darlene had used her nickname. "Are you all right?" She moved closer.

"I'm fine," she croaked.

"You're sure now?" Darlene didn't seem to believe her.

"Very sure. I was concentrating so hard on the computer screen I didn't hear you." *He's gone!* something inside screamed. *He's gone.* She couldn't believe it. She was surprised at the sound of her own voice when she spoke again. "I thought he wanted this information to take with him. I was trying to finish it."

"He does. He wants me to bring it to the airport at two o'clock. Will that be okay for you?"

"Fine." *Go, Darlene, please go. I want to scream and I can't scream with you in front of me.* "I'll bring it to you when I'm done."

Mercifully, she left. Nikki rose from her chair like a

dead thing, walked to the door, and locked it. She went back to her desk, put her head in her hands, and began a serious, heartbreaking weep. He hadn't even said goodbye.

In a few minutes, she began fighting for a vestige of control. She lifted her head, her red eyes turned to the door between her office and the boardroom. With all her heart, her soul, she was wishing Darlene was wrong, that Michael was on the other side. She could see him there, sitting at the table, jacket off, shirt-sleeves pushed back. When she went in, he would look up and smile. She would go to him, tell him it was all a mistake. She loved him, wanted him. Nikki got up, went to the door, and opened it. The room was empty.

Nikki could feel the tears again, thickening behind her eyelids. She had to get out of here, out of this damned place. She couldn't breathe.

Along with everybody else in the office, Amy saw Nikki walk from her office, her face tight with control, her head high. Mascara rivers ran down her waxen face, and there was a big smudge of eye shadow on her right cheek. Amy stood up to go to her.

Nikki lifted a hand. "Don't say anything, Amy. Not a word. At the moment, I'm held together by a single thread. Do me a favor, will you? Cancel my day. I've already managed to cancel my life."

Amy nodded. When Darlene had told her Michael wasn't coming in today, she knew it would be difficult for Nikki. Why was she so stubborn? she thought. Michael was incredible and so much in love with her. Amy didn't understand it, didn't understand it at all. Her hazel eyes were soft with compassion when she looked into her friend's cheerless face.

"Will you be back at all?" she asked.

"Don't count on it. Right now, I can't face this place."

"Niks—" Amy started.

Nikki interrupted. "I'll be okay. I just don't want to talk about it. Okay?"

"Okay. But call me later."

"All right." Nikki turned to go.

"Promise?"

"I promise."

Michael sat in a bar at the Vancouver International Airport. Any other time he would be in the V.I.P. lounge, thankful for the quiet and privacy to work, rest, or make a few last-minute phone calls. Not today. Today the crowded, noisy bar suited him. He needed the distraction. There was nothing like a busy airport to provide that. He sat near the front of the bar and rarely took his eyes off its broad entrance. Again he looked at his watch.

He rubbed a hand over its antique dial. It had been his father's watch and his father before him, and it was the only physical remembrance he had of him. He wondered how many times the men of the Dorado family had looked at this same watch as they waited for that special woman. For his grandfather and his father that woman had come. Would he be so lucky?

Nikki arrived back at the office shortly before one o'clock. She had walked, wept, walked again, wept again, and finally decided to go back to work. For one thing she was feeling guilty. The least she could do was make sure Darlene had all the reports Michael requested. During her wilder moments of the last few hours, she had toyed with taking them to him herself. She had talked herself out of it. She would be the last person he would want to see. And she couldn't face his distantly friendly manner. The pain would be too great. She could see him taking the reports from her, thanking her graciously, and extending his firm hand to say goodbye. No. She would not put herself through that.

She crossed the open office area to her own door. The office was empty. It would fill up again in a few minutes when the secretaries and sales staff returned from lunch. For now, Nikki was glad of the calm, glad she didn't have to face too many questioning eyes. She knew she'd been a spectacle when she'd left. What stories were circulating about the general manager's crying jag, she could only guess. Right now, she didn't care.

She slipped into her own office, closed the door, and headed automatically to her desk. Engrossed in reading a sheaf of pink telephone messages, she didn't look up until she was almost to her chair. Then she saw it.

A single white rose in an exquisite crystal vase. Propped at its base was a card. She hesitated before reaching for it, her breath arrested, caught somewhere near her heart. Then, with a trembling hand, she picked up the envelope and opened it. Only then did her breath and her life return.

My darling Nikki,
Remember the roses? I will be in the Island Lounge at the airport until flight time. Don't come unless you plan to marry me. I love you.
Michael

Nikki blinked as she looked at the card and its bold signature. Although she would have sworn there were no more left, tears again swelled in her eyes. Delicately, she fingered the petals of the perfect ivory rose. She closed her eyes, still caressing the delicate flower. "White for love's pure light," he'd said. She remembered. Could she ever forget?

She crushed the flower to her breast and lifted her eyes.

Michael saw her coming before she saw him. He stood to greet her, his heart pounding, his body weak with relief.

In seconds, she was in his arms. He tightened his grip as heart beat against heart. He would never, never let her go again. He held her from him and took her face in his hands.

"I wasn't sure you'd come," he said simply.

"I thought . . . that morning in the office . . . after our weekend together— You were so calm, Michael, so unshakably cool and I . . ." She paused. "I was a mess, confused, afraid . . . and so much in love with you I . . . I didn't know what to do."

He brought her tight to his chest, his hand cradling her head against his shoulder. "What you did, love, was scare the hell out of me."

She pulled her head back to look into the deep green of his eyes. Her own were bright with tears. She tried to speak but couldn't and again buried her face in his broad, welcoming chest. There were no words. No words at all. It was Michael who spoke.

"You'll marry me then?" He whispered the words into her ear. Again she pulled back, her smile brilliant.

"I have to," she said. "In the last few hours, I discovered that I couldn't live without you. You've given me no choice, Mr. Dorado. No choice at all."

"I didn't intend to."

"I'll still want to work, Michael, and I'd like to stay with Prisma. There must be something I can do. Some way we can work it out." She looked up at him, her face a mixture of love, worry, and determination.

"You can have my job. I only used it so I could

have my way with you. Now that I see my days as an office Romeo are over, I won't need it anymore."

"Michael!"

"Hush. This is not the time or the place to show me how grateful you are. Besides, I've got a plane to catch, remember?"

Nikki kissed him then, oblivious to the smiles and stares they were getting from the crowded bar. The kiss was long, deep, and breathless, and she ended it with a question.

"Is there anything I can do that would make you miss that plane?"

Michael picked up his briefcase, put an arm around her, and smiled. "You could . . . take me skiing."

After all, the skies were full of planes.

SHARE THE FUN . . .
SHARE YOUR NEW-FOUND TREASURE!!

You don't want to let your new books out of your sight?
That's okay. Your friends can get their own. Order below.

No. 89 JUST ONE KISS by Carole Dean
Michael is Nikki's guardian angel and too handsome for his own good.

No. 1 ALWAYS by Catherine Sellers
A modern day "knight in shining armor." Forever . . . for always!

No. 2 NO HIDING PLACE by Brooke Sinclair
Pretty government agent & handsome professor = mystery & romance.

No. 3 SOUTHERN HOSPITALITY by Sally Falcon
North meets South. War is declared. Both sides win!!!

No. 4 WINTERFIRE by Lois Faye Dyer
Beautiful NY model and rugged Idaho rancher find their own magic.

No. 5 A LITTLE INCONVENIENCE by Judy Christenberry
Liz faces every obstacle Jason throws at her—even his love.

No. 6 CHANGE OF PACE by Sharon Brondos
Can Sam protect himself from Deirdre, the green-eyed temptress?

No. 7 SILENT ENCHANTMENT by Lacey Dancer
Was she real? She was Alex's true-to-life fairy tale princess.

No. 8 STORM WARNING by Kathryn Brocato
Passion raged out of their control—and there was no warning!

No. 9 PRODIGAL LOVER by Margo Gregg
Bryan is a mystery. Could he be Keely's presumed dead husband?

No. 10 FULL STEAM by Cassie Miles
Jonathan's a dreamer—Darcy is practical. An unlikely combo!

No. 11 BY THE BOOK by Christine Dorsey
Charlotte and Mac give parent-teacher conference a new meaning.

No. 12 BORN TO BE WILD by Kris Cassidy
Jenny shouldn't get close to Garrett. He'll leave too, won't he?

No. 13 SIEGE OF THE HEART by Sheryl McDanel Munson
Nick pursues Court while she wrestles with her heart and mind.

No. 14 TWO FOR ONE by Phyllis Herrmann
What is it about Cal and Elliot that has Leslie seeing double?

No. 15 A MATTER OF TIME by Ann Bullard
Does Josh *really* want Christine or is there something else?

No. 16 FACE TO FACE by Shirley Faye
Christi's definitely not Damon's type. So, what's the attraction?

No. 17 OPENING ACT by Ann Patrick
Big city playwright meets small town sheriff and life heats up.

No. 18 RAINBOW WISHES by Jacqueline Case
Mason is looking for more from life. Evie may be his pot of gold!

No. 19 SUNDAY DRIVER by Valerie Kane
Carrie breaks through all Cam's defenses showing him how to love.

No. 20 CHEATED HEARTS by Karen Lawton Barrett
T.C. and Lucas find their way back into each other's hearts.

No. 21 THAT JAMES BOY by Lois Faye Dyer
Jesse believes in love at first sight. Will he convince Sarah?

No. 22 NEVER LET GO by Laura Phillips
Ryan has a big dilemma. Kelly is the answer to *all* his prayers.

No. 23 A PERFECT MATCH by Susan Combs
Ross can keep Emily safe but can he save himself from Emily?

Meteor Publishing Corporation
Dept. 593, P. O. Box 41820, Philadelphia, PA 19101-9828

Please send the books I've indicated below. Check or money order (U.S. Dollars only)—no cash, stamps or C.O.D.s (PA residents, add 6% sales tax). I am enclosing $2.95 plus 75¢ handling fee for *each* book ordered.

Total Amount Enclosed: $_____.

____ No. 89	____ No. 6	____ No. 12	____ No. 18
____ No. 1	____ No. 7	____ No. 13	____ No. 19
____ No. 2	____ No. 8	____ No. 14	____ No. 20
____ No. 3	____ No. 9	____ No. 15	____ No. 21
____ No. 4	____ No. 10	____ No. 16	____ No. 22
____ No. 5	____ No. 11	____ No. 17	____ No. 23

Please Print:
Name _____
Address _____ Apt. No. _____
City/State _____ Zip _____

Allow four to six weeks for delivery. Quantities limited.